ELEMENTS OF CHEMISTRY

ATTRACTION (PART 1)

PENNY REID

To the figurative Bunsen Burner in pants everywhere.

[1]

ATOMS, MOLECULES, AND IONS

Q*UIET, SILENT, MUTED, hushed, stilled, reticent…* I moved my mouth, breathed the words—soundlessly—from my hiding place.

This game comforted me, calmed me, settled my nerves. Yes, recalling synonyms while anxious was a bizarre coping strategy, but it worked. And very little usually worked.

The voices from beyond the cabinet grew louder and were accompanied by the click of heels and the dull echo of tennis shoes. I held my breath and strained to decipher how many sets of feet were represented by the approaching shoes. I guessed two, also because only two voices were audible.

"…think that he's going to want to fuck you? After what happened last Friday?" The words were a hiss emanating from an unknown male voice; I tensed at the use of vulgarity.

"I'll get there late. If you do your job then he won't even remember it," came a feminine reply. The female was closest to my hiding spot in the chemistry lab cabinet; her words were, therefore, much clearer.

"Shit," he said. I tried not to huff in disgust at his foul language as he continued. "I don't even know how much to use. I've only used it on bitches."

1

"I don't know either. Just…double it. Martin is, what? Like, twice the size of the girls you usually dope out?"

I tensed again, my eyes narrowing. The name Martin, in particular, made my heart beat faster. I knew only one Martin.

Martin Sandeke.

Martin Sandeke, the heir to Sandeke Telecom Systems in Palo Alto, California, and smartypants in his own right. I also came from a notable family—my mother was a US senator, my father was the dean of the college of medicine at UCLA, and my maternal grandfather was an astronaut. However, unlike Martin's family, we weren't billionaires. We were scientists, politicians, and scholars.

Martin Sandeke, the six-foot-three modern day physical manifestation of Hercules and captain of our university's rowing team.

Martin Sandeke, unrepentant manwhore extraordinaire and kind of a jerk-faced bully.

Martin Sandeke, my year-long chemistry lab partner and all-around most unobtainable person in the universe—who I never spoke to except to ask for beakers, relay findings, and request modifications to the heat level of my Bunsen burner.

And by Bunsen burner I meant, literally, my Bunsen burner. Not the figurative Bunsen burner in my pants. Because I hoped Martin Sandeke had no idea that he affected the heat levels of my figurative Bunsen burner.

He did affect them. But, obviously—since he was cosmically unobtainable and kind of a bully—I didn't want him to know that.

"He's about two twenty, so…yeah. I guess," the male responded. His tennis shoes made scuffing sounds on the linoleum as he neared my hiding spot.

I rolled my lips between my teeth and stared at the crack in the cabinet doors. I couldn't see his face, but I could now discern he was standing directly in front of the cabinet, next to the unknown girl. Maybe facing her.

"But what's in it for me?" the cuss monster asked, his voice lower than it had been, more intimate.

I heard some rustling then the sloppy sounds of kissing. Instinctively, I stuck my tongue out and mocked gagging. Listening to public displays of affection was unpleasant, especially when lip smacking and groaning was involved, and most especially while trapped in a chemistry lab cabinet that smelled heavily of sulfur.

The next words spoken came from the girl and were a bit whiny. "Money, dummy. Martin's loaded—well, his family is loaded—and they'll buy me off. All you have to do is give him the stuff tonight in his drink. I'll take him upstairs, record the whole thing. Bonus if I get pregnant."

My mouth dropped open, my eyes wide, unable to believe what I'd just heard. The awfulness, rustling, and lip smacking continued.

"You dope him and I'll rope him." The girl's pleasure-filled gasps were audible and rather ridiculous sounding.

"Oh, yeah baby—touch me there." These breathy words were accompanied by the sound of a beaker crashing to the ground and a zipper being undone.

I winced, scowled. Really, people had no manners or sense of decorum.

"No, no, we can't. He'll be here any minute. I need to leave," the girl pleaded. I noted she sounded the perfect mixture of regretful and hurried. "You need to make sure he stays at the house for the party. I'll be there at eleven, so give him the stuff around ten thirty, okay?"

The zipper came back up, the man backed into the cabinet. I jerked at the resultant bang of the doors. "How do you know where he'll be all the time?"

"We dated, remember?"

"No. He fucked you. You never dated. Martin Sandeke doesn't date."

"Yeah, well, I know his schedule. He comes here on Fridays and does…hell if I know what with his ugly little lab partner."

Ugly?

I twisted my lips to the side, my heart seized in my chest.

I hated the word ugly. It was an ugly word.

*Ugly, unsightly, gross, misshapen, repelling…*I mentally recited. For some reason, the synonym game didn't help me this time.

"His lab partner? Wait, I've heard about her. Isn't her dad an astronaut, or something?"

"Who cares? She's nobody. Kathy or Kelly or something. Whatever," the girl huffed, the heels of her shoes carrying her farther away. "Forget about her, she's nothing. The point is you need to stay here and make sure he comes tonight, okay? I gotta go before he gets here."

"Bitch, you better not be playing me."

The girl responded but I didn't catch the words. My back itched and while tucked in the cabinet, I couldn't reach the spot. In fact, it would be a difficult spot to reach even if I were standing in an open field. Also, my mind was still reciting synonyms for ugly.

I didn't think I was *ugly*.

I knew my hair was unremarkable. It was long, wavy, and dark brown. I always wore it in a ponytail, bun, or clip. This was because hair, other than warming my head, served no purpose. Mostly, I ignored it.

I rather liked my eyes. They were grey. It was an unusual color I'd been told on more than one occasion. Granted, no one ever said they were pretty, but no one ever said they were *ugly* either. That had to count for something.

I was no supermodel in height or size, at five foot seven and a size ten. But I wasn't Jabba the Hut either.

My teeth were reasonably straight, though I had a noticeable gap between the front top two. I was also pale—the color of paper my best friend, Sam, had once said. My eyebrows were too thick, I knew this. Sam—short for Samantha—often remarked that I should get them plucked, thinned out.

I ignored this advice, as I didn't care about thick eyebrows so long as they never became a unibrow like my aunt Viki's.

I glanced down at my comfortable clothes—men's wide-leg, navy cargo pants with torn-off cuffs, worn Converse, and an oversized Weezer T-shirt. I might be plain, unremarkable, or even mousy. But it's not like I was a horrible beast who turned people into stone with a single gaze. I was just…low maintenance.

That was okay with me. I didn't need attention, didn't want it.

People, especially people my age and especially other girls, made very little sense to me. I didn't see the value in spending hours in front of a mirror when I could be playing video games, or playing the guitar, or reading a book instead.

But sometimes, when I was with Martin and we were calculating particulate levels, I wanted to be beautiful. Really, it was the only time I wished I looked different. Then I remembered he was a jerk-face and everything went back to normal.

I gave myself a mental shake and gritted my teeth. Straining to listen, I pressed my ear against the cabinet door and waited for signs the unknown male was still present.

The itch in the center of my back was spreading and I didn't know how much longer I could stand it. On the itch scale, it was quickly moving from aggravating to brain-exploding torturous.

But then the sound of shuffling footsteps approaching from the hall snagged my attention. They slowed, then stopped.

"Hey man. Whatsup?" said the mystery cussing fiend.

"What are you doing here?" Martin asked. I guessed he was standing at the entrance to the lab because his voice was somewhat muffled. Regardless, it made my stomach erupt in rabid butterflies. I often had a physical response to the sound of Martin's voice.

"Wanted to make sure you're coming to the house party tonight."

I heard more footsteps. They were Martin's. I'd know that nonchalant gait anywhere—because I was pathetic and maybe a little obsessed with all things Martin Sandeke. But the difference between my obsession with Martin and the other girls' obsession with Martin was that I had absolutely no problem admiring his finer features from afar.

Because Martin really was kind of a jerk.

He'd never been a jerk to me, likely because I was an excellent lab partner. We spoke only about chemistry—and he liked acing assignments—but I'd seen him in action. He'd lose his temper and then *BOOM!* he'd go off on whatever poor soul he happened to believe responsible.

If it was a girl, they'd leave crying after coming in contact with his razor wit (and, by razor, I mean cutting and wound inducing). He never called them names, he didn't have to. He'd just tell them the truth.

If it was a guy, he *might* only use words. But sometimes he used fists too. I'd been a witness to this once—Martin beating the crap out of a slightly shorter but also slightly broader jilted boyfriend of one of his one-night stands. At least, that was the rumor that went around after both of them were escorted out of the dining hall by campus police.

Martin was an equal opportunity jerk-face and therefore best avoided outside of the chemistry lab.

No one spoke for a moment; then, I stiffened when I heard Martin ask, "Where's Parker?"

That was me. I'm Parker.

To be more precise, I'm Kaitlyn Parker, Katy for short; but I doubt Martin knows my first name.

"Parker? Who's Parker?"

"My lab partner."

"I thought your lab partner was that girl, the one—"

"She is a girl."

"Her name is Parker?"

I knew Martin was close now because I heard him sigh; his next words were clipped with impatience. "What did you want again?"

"The party tonight—you're still coming, right?"

"I already told you I'd be there."

"Good. Because I'm counting on you to be my wingman." The mystery speaker's voice started to fade. I guessed he was leaving, having secured what he came for.

"Yeah, whatever," was Martin's offhanded response.

"I'll see you tonight, bro. You better come, I'm serious."

Martin didn't respond. I guessed the unknown male finally exited because, after a silent pause, I heard Martin release a very audible huff. It was heavy, exaggerated, and flavored with exasperation; of note, I'd heard him employ this sigh once before with a girl who followed him into our chemistry lab. I never wanted to be on the receiving end of that sigh—so far so good.

Meanwhile, I was still in the chemistry cabinet and the itch of the century had spread to my shoulders and stomach. I was likely going to go crazy if I didn't scratch it within the next ten seconds. It felt like I was being repeatedly stung by a legion of fire ants.

During those ten seconds I debated my options.

I could stay in the cabinet, wait for Martin to leave, go quietly insane, then send him an anonymous note about the conversation I'd overheard.

Or, I could burst forth from my hiding place, scratch my itch, look like the doofus I was, then hope he'd forget as I regaled him with details of the conversation I'd overheard.

In the end it didn't matter, because the cabinet doors were abruptly opened. A whoosh of fresh air followed and I found myself face-to-face with Martin Sandeke.

His eyes were blue and exceptionally beautiful. They reminded me of blue flame. Well, usually they were lovely, at present they were narrowed and sharp, and focused squarely on me. Beginning with my eyes, they moved down then up, ending where they started.

He was truly a magnificent specimen. All broad shoulders and narrow hips, with the thick muscular thighs of a rower. His brown hair was streaked with blond—likely due to all his time on the water and in the sun.

I wasn't used to this—him looking *at* me, standing so close—thus, combined with my normal female palpitations, I couldn't quite draw breath for several seconds.

At length he said, "Parker."

"Sandeke."

"What are you doing?"

"Uh…" I released the breath I'd been holding and unthinkingly arched my back, reaching behind me to scratch my itch.

Maybe it was the effect of his eyes and unavoidable handsome-ness, or maybe it was because I'd seen him rip girls to shreds and was therefore a little afraid of a potential non-chemistry related conversation. Or maybe it was the itch between my shoulder blades, because without thinking, I blurted the truth, "I was hiding in the cabinet."

His brow furrowed, but his gaze relaxed slightly, his confusion plain. "Why are you hiding in the cabinet?"

I reached over my shoulder, stretching my arm, and tried to reach the itch with my left hand instead of my right. This didn't work.

"Why does anyone hide in a chemistry cabinet?" I shrugged, mostly because I hoped the movement would help me get to the itch.

He lifted a single eyebrow and grabbed me by my upper arms, pulling and lifting me like I weighed next to nothing. He set me safely on the ground.

Martin's hands on my arms sent a bolt of girly awareness to the pit of my stomach. It was paired with belated embarrassment at being found as a burst of heat spread from my chest to my neck.

He still gripped my arms when he asked, "Do you hide in the cabinet often?"

"Sometimes," I said distractedly, my jaw clenched, willing the mortified blush to recede.

"Is this an everyday thing?"

"No. Only on special occasions, like when strange people arrive to plot your demise." I twisted out of his grip, reached for and failed to find the spot needed to secure relief.

"Plot my demise?" His eyes darted over me again, I could tell he was studying my movements. "What are you doing?"

"Trying to reach an itch between my shoulder blades." My elbow was in the air now, my hand down the neck of my shirt.

Martin's eyes widened then blinked. Without a word he stepped forward into my personal space. Before I could comprehend what was happening, he'd backed me into the lab table and I was trapped. Martin was against me, his arms wrapped around my body, his hands slipped under my T-shirt to the center of my back, and then his fingers itched the unreachable space between my shoulder blades.

At first I tensed because... *MARTIN SANDEKE'S ARMS ARE AROUND ME. HIS HANDS ARE UNDER MY SHIRT. HIS BODY IS PRESSED AGAINST MINE!*

OMG. WTF? BBQ!

But then, my brain's very understandably stunted fan-girl reaction to his movements was quickly eclipsed by the blissful relief of an itch scratched.

I melted in his arms, my forehead resting against his chest, and I moaned my satisfaction.

"Oh, yes, God. That's the spot… Please, don't stop," I murmured, obviously out of my mind. But it felt so good. So very, very good. Like sinking into a hot bubble bath after walking a mile through a nor'easter.

Martin didn't stop.

Well…not precisely.

Rather, over the course of a full minute, he ceased using his nails, and instead began caressing and massaging my back with his fingers and hands. I realized too late that his head had dipped to my neck and his lips were against my ear, his hot breath tickling me and sending delightfully dangerous shivers down my spine, and down the backs of my legs to my toes.

"Did I make it all better?" he whispered, then bit—yes, bit!—my neck, like he was tasting me.

Then he bit me again.

I sucked in a breath and my eyes opened—even as my body instinctively arched toward him. Reality burst through the delightful fog of his ministrations like one of those disturbing and jarring windup jack-in-the-box clowns.

After one and a half semesters of virtually nothing but mundane academic interactions, I was in the chemistry lab with Martin Sandeke and his hands were roaming, liberal, and greedy. His face was tucked in my neck. I was trapped against a lab table. Our bodies were intimately connected.

And I'd just moaned.

What the hiccup was going on?

I raised my palms to his chest and made to push him away. This only caused his hands to still, now on the curve of my waist, and his grip to tighten. He plastered our fronts together more completely.

"Um…" I cleared my throat, found my voice unsteady. "Yeah, yeah —all better," I croaked.

He laughed. Actually, it was more like a lazy chuckle.

One of Martin's hands slipped up my back and under the strap of my bra, where the itch had been, his fingers splayed wide. The other went to the clip on my head and released the spring. My hair fell like a curtain and I felt him wrap his hand around the thick length.

I pushed him again, tilted my head to the side and away, feeling breathless. "I'm all better now. Thanks for the help. Services no longer needed." Everywhere he touched sent ripples of awareness and heat to my core.

My attempt at escape was a failure, because, as soon as I pressed against him in earnest, Martin tugged my hair, encouraging me to tilt my chin upward.

Then he kissed me.

And—damn, damn, damn—he was a good kisser.

More precisely, since I had grossly limited experience in the kissing department, he was what I imagined a good kisser would kiss like. The kind girls fantasize about. The guy who just takes what he wants, like he's hungry and you're on the menu, but somehow makes it epic for both parties involved.

No preamble, prologue, or preface. Just urgent, fervent, worshipful kisses, one right after the other. I had no choice but to wrap my arms around his neck, stand on my tiptoes, and try to kiss him back. Because, honestly, the way he held me, the way he growled when our tongues met, the way his mouth moved over mine—he demanded it.

Also, in the recesses of my mind, I realized that this entire situation was completely preposterous. Likely, he was drunk, or tripping on acid, or was playing some kind of joke.

One day I would persuade my grandchildren to gather 'round while I put in my good dentures—the ones with no space between my two front teeth—and I would tell them for the millionth time about how Hercules had once accidentally kissed me in the chemistry lab at my Ivy League University.

The need for air eventually required our lips to part, though we separated only inches. If I inclined my head forward our noses would touch.

I opened my eyes as wide as they would go and glanced at his, where I found his gaze alternately moving between my lips and my eyes. I also noted I wasn't the only one breathing heavily.

I said and thought in unison, my voice just above a whisper, "What was that?"

His eyes stopped moving over my face and instead settled, held mine captive. They were heated and…hot and…intense. I was starting to understand why the blood of a thousand virgins had been sacrificed at his altar of sexual prowess.

I tried to swallow. I couldn't.

"That was necessary," he finally said. Actually, he growled it.

"Necessary?"

"Yes. That needed to happen."

"It did?"

He nodded once and bent as though he were going to do it again. I stiffened, my hands moved instantly to his chest and I thwarted his advance—because, if he started kissing me, it was surely a sign of Armageddon. Also, I was so far out of my comfort level, I was in an alternate dimension.

"No-no-no-no." I twisted my head to the side, braced my hands against the imposing wall of his chest. "We're not doing that again. I don't kiss unobtainable boys, it's one of my life rules."

He tugged my hair—I'd forgotten that he'd wrapped his hand around it—and bodily pressed me against the black-topped lab table. His other arm, still under my shirt, wrapped completely around me.

"Yes. We're doing *that* again."

"No. We're not. We're not doing anything unless it involves measuring the composition of trace elements in surface water."

"Parker—" His hand left my hair and slipped under my shirt again, spanning my side and stomach.

"Because we're lab partners and lab partners do not kiss."

"Then we're not lab partners anymore."

"You can't switch lab partners in the middle of the semester."

"I just did."

My fingers moved to catch his wrists because his hands were on their way to second base; I successfully intercepted his northward progress. "Nope. I don't do that."

"Do what?" He nuzzled my neck and whispered against my skin. He must've known that nuzzling was going to cause my insides to melt. I imagined he'd conducted methodical experiments into the fastest way to female self-lubrication.

"I'm not one of your easy girls, or even difficult girls." My voice wavered, so I cleared my throat. "I'm not even really a girl. I'm more like one of the boys. Think of me like a boy."

"Not possible."

"It's true. Do you kiss boys? Because, if not, then I think you must have me confused with someone else."

His movements stilled and a long moment passed. Then his hands fell away, *he* stepped away, and I slumped slightly forward—a weird mixture of feeling bereft and relieved.

"You're a lesbian." He said the words as though they explained a mystery he'd been trying to solve for years.

My eyes shot to his. He was four feet away and I found him watching me with a dawning of... something. If I didn't know any better it looked like disappointment and frustration.

I swallowed, successfully, licked my lips, then shook my head. The irony of his confusion not lost on me.

My first and only boyfriend had been gay. I just didn't know it while we were dating throughout high school.

I was still trying to catch my breath when I responded, "No. I'm not gay. I'm just...not interested in you that way."

This was true—because I'd witnessed his path of devastation with my own eyes.

This was also a lie—because I was most definitely interested in him *that* way, just not the after part where he would say it was meaningless sex, make me cry, and tell me to get over it.

His eyebrows jumped a fraction of a centimeter at my softly spoken declaration.

"Not interested...," he repeated.

I stepped to the side, scaling the length of the table, and reached for my bag. I hefted it to my shoulder, escape now the only thing on my mind. His slightly narrowed eyes followed my movements.

"I know, right?" I tried to sound self-deprecating, which wasn't difficult because I truly meant my next words. "Who am I? I'm nobody."

"You're not nobody," he countered. "Your mother is a senator and your grandfather was an astronaut."

I cringed. I hated it when people brought up my family. "Just because my family is famous, doesn't mean I'm somebody."

He shifted forward and said with a surprising amount of vehemence. "Exactly! That's exactly right."

"I know, right?" I readily agreed. "See, I'm ordinary. And you're you and I'm sure you're used to the deafening sound of underwear hitting the floor every time you enter a room. But I don't do that kind of thing, even for Hercules. Sure, I'll think about the possibility later when I'm safely alone in bed, but I never cross-pollinate fantasy and reality."

"When you're alone in bed?"

I didn't acknowledge his words because…mortification.

Instead, I said, "I'm not a fast and loose girl. I'm a slow and steady girl. Who knows when or if I'll ever cross the finish line?"

He blinked at me, at my deluge of words. I didn't even try to read his expression because I was so focused on walking backward out of the room.

"You're leaving?" he asked.

"Yep." I threw my thumb over my shoulder. "I'm going to go now. And don't worry about the experiment. I'll come in over spring break and finish it up. And when I see you after the break, everything will be back to normal. We can forget this ever happened. We shall never speak of it." My voice cracked on the last word.

"Parker—"

"Have a really great spring break."

"Kaitlyn—" He took two strides forward as though he were going to stop me, but halted at the sound of crunching glass underfoot. He glanced at his feet, noticing for the first time the broken beaker on the floor. "What the hell?"

I seized the opportunity afforded by his split attention and bolted out of the room.

In fact, I ran down the hall like an insane person and slipped into the elevator just before it closed. I even jogged back to my dorm, didn't begin to relax until I crossed the threshold of the keycard access area, climbed the three flights to my room, and locked the door behind me.

I tossed my bag to the corner of the tiny space, threw myself backward on my bed, and rubbed my eyes with the base of my palms. The scene in the lab played over and over behind my closed eyelids—him touching me, kissing me, scratching the impossible itch.

It wasn't until several minutes later that I realized I'd forgotten to tell him about the dastardly plot I'd overheard.

[2]

THE ATOMIC THEORY OF MATTER

"I CAN'T BELIEVE you agreed to this."

"Shut it, Sam."

I tucked my long, straightened-with-a-flatiron brown hair behind my ears. Self-consciously, I smoothed the skirt of the little black dress she'd talked me into wearing, annoyed—for the twentieth time—that the hem of the skirt ended mid-thigh.

"You look hot, hooker. Just own it." Sam nudged my elbow with hers and I grimaced.

If someone had asked me twelve hours ago how I'd be spending the first Friday night of spring break, I would have told them I'd be curled up in my bed against fluffy pillows, sipping tea, and eating shortbread while reading.

I would not and could not have fathomed I'd be on my way to a fraternity party dressed in lace-topped thigh highs, a black dress, stiletto heels, with my hair down, *and* wearing makeup.

That's right. Makeup. On my face. With glitter eye shadow.

Also, my eyebrows were plucked. *Plucked!* Gah!

I rolled my eyes and huffed like the disgruntled recluse I was. I would rather shop for a bra than go to a fraternity party, and that was saying a lot.

"Oh, come on, Katy. There was no way we could get into the party wearing band T-shirts and men's pants. This is a skirts-only party."

I'd been educated earlier in the evening that a "skirts-only party" is a fraternity party where all the girls are required to wear short skirts. Upon hearing this news I briefly considered leaving Martin to his fate. In the end, my conscience wouldn't let me.

Jerk conscience. Always making me do things.

"You act like getting dressed up is torture," she continued. "You look hot." Sam, who I suspected had been waiting for a chance like this since our freshman year of high school, didn't sound at all sorry for me.

"I don't look hot. I look ridiculous."

"You're a babe."

"Shut it."

"A hot babe. And guys are going to be wanting some of that." She pointed at me and flicked her wrist, indicating my bosom and backside. "Especially 'dat ass."

I grumbled, but made no other audible response. Inwardly, I cursed myself for the hundredth time that I'd failed to warn Martin about the plot I'd overheard in the chemistry lab earlier. If I'd just kept my wits about me I would be curled up with a book now instead of walking toward a den of inequity dressed like a girl.

Even though we were still two blocks away, I could hear the sounds of the party. My neck felt stiff and my hands were clammy.

The plan was quite simple. I would find Martin, explain about the plot and what I'd overheard, then we would leave. Sam wasn't a frat party kind of girl either. Yes, she liked to get dressed up, but she called sorority girls "sorostitutes" and fraternity guys "fratilos." She labeled them "group thinkers" and claimed they suffered from a herd mentality.

She was kind of judgey that way.

I hadn't given sororities or fraternities much thought because...no point.

"I still don't get why you don't have his cell number. He's your lab partner, right? And he was your lab partner last semester too?" Sam tossed her blonde curls over her shoulder.

Sam was a little shorter than me and was attending the University on a tennis scholarship. She was determined to get into Harvard Law and, therefore like me, she was focused, spent very little of her time looking for ways to sow oats. Her all-business attitude made her an ideal best friend and roommate.

"I just don't. I don't have his number."

"Why not?" she pressed. She'd asked me this question several times as we were dressing—or, rather, as she was dressing me.

"Because," I responded again, wiping my palms on the dress.

"Because why? What if you needed to get in touch with him about a project?"

"I'd leave him a note."

"A note? Where? When? How?"

"In the chemistry lab, in the cabinet."

"You pass each other notes?" Her tone turned teasing.

"No. It's not like that. I'll leave a note if I can't make it on Fridays and he does the same. Or, if I've finished something without waiting for him, that kind of thing."

"But why didn't he want you to have his cell—"

I stopped walking and faced her. "He tried to give it to me, okay? He tried last semester to exchange numbers and I didn't want to. Can you just drop it?"

"You wouldn't take Martin Sandeke's number?" she asked, as though the words I'd just spoken made no sense.

"That's correct."

"But...why the hell not? He's...he's...he's Martin Sandeke!"

"*Because* he's Martin Sandeke. That's why I wouldn't take it." I started walking again, my toes protesting the movement.

"Katy, you've been crushing on Martin Sandeke since the first week of class two years ago when you stalked him outside of physics, before you even knew who he was."

"That's because he's physically beautiful and pleasing to the eye," I mumbled.

"He tries to give you his phone number and you don't take it. Why did you do that? Explain it to me."

"Because, you know me, when I get drunk—even though it's only happened twice—I drunk dial! I called Carter the last time it happened."

Carter was my high school boyfriend who never seemed interested in physical intimacy unless we had an audience. Since he was my only boyfriend, I figured this was normal. We'd parted as friends.

But last year I left him a drunk message asking him why he never tried to sleep with me. When I woke up the next morning, and everything came flooding back, it took me three weeks to return his call.

When I finally did, he informed me that he was, in fact, gay. Additionally, he had appreciated my willingness to be his beard in high school. He also assured me that had he not been gay, he would have tried to get in my pants early and often.

It all sounded like pity.

Worst conversation ever.

Sam stopped me again with a hand on my elbow. "That was last summer and Carter is ancient history."

"Can we just get this over with?" I pleaded, not wanting to talk about Carter or about my stunted romantic history.

Sam released an audible breath. "Katy, you're beautiful and desirable—"

"Oh my God, no more teasing. I'm wearing the dress, aren't I? I even let you put makeup on me."

"I'm not teasing you. I'm trying to get you out of this perpetual funk you're in. You hide yourself behind baggy clothes and eyebrows so thick they could be mustaches. Carter is a lovely person but he shouldn't have used you like that. Now you're all skewed in the head."

"Can we not talk about this?"

"Only if you promise to get Martin's number tonight."

I shook my head, shifted on my feet. "I will not. I don't want to drunk dial Martin Sandeke a few months from now. He won't give me pity, he's vicious. He'll laugh in my face and make me cry."

Sam *tsked,* rolled her eyes, and started walking again. "Fine. Whatever. Go through life repressing your sexuality because one boy—one stupid boy who was confused—used you to hide his own inner turmoil."

"Thank you."

"You're not welcome."

I let her snarky comment slide because we were on the same block as the fraternity house.

It was what one would expect from a fraternity house at an Ivy League school. Large, several stories, classically painted, manicured lawn littered with red solo cups and drunk partygoers. The mass of bodies—standing, sitting, leaning—spilled out the front door, down the sweeping staircase, and onto the grass.

At the entrance to the house stood two very large men. Actually, I got the distinct impression they were bouncer dudes. Both were dressed in fraternity polo shirts and their necks were as thick as my waist. They were chatting up a group of five, tall, sylphlike girls. Their eyes scanned both Sam and me when we mounted the ginormous wrap-around porch.

In front of us, two girls in jeans and a guy—also in jeans—began crossing the threshold of the house.

"What do you think you're doing?" One of the big dudes held his hand out and halted their progress.

The shorter of the two jean-clad girls shrugged and faced the big dude. "Goin' to the party."

"Nah-uh, this is a skirts-only party."

The second big dude tipped his chin toward Sam and me. "You can go in, girls."

Sam pushed me gently on my shoulder and we moved around the group stalled at the entrance. Once inside, Sam and I wove through bodies; I had no idea where we were going or how I was going to find Martin.

Looking around, I started to feel a bit better about my dress. It was black cotton, sleeveless, and shorter than I thought appropriate, but it was modest in comparison to some of the dresses and miniskirts we saw as we entered the gigantic entryway.

I did not, however, feel better about the crowd. People, people everywhere; dancing, making out, arguing, drinking, laughing. Even given the mammoth size of the foyer, the crush felt suffocating.

"Excuse me."

I stepped to the side to allow three tall and handsome guys brush past. They looked almost interchangeable—intentionally long brown hair cut in the hipster style, tanned skin; two of them had brown eyes, the other one had blue. They were wearing fraternity polo shirts and all three slowed, their eyes moving over Sam and me with plain interest.

The last of the guys stopped; he grabbed my hips, then issued me a very cute and flirty grin. "Hey, who are you?"

I opened my mouth to respond that I was nobody and that he shouldn't go around touching people without their permission, but Sam tugged on my hand and inserted herself into the conversation. She had to semi-yell in order to be heard over the surrounding music and voices. "We're looking for Martin Sandeke. Is he here?"

The blue-eyed one of the trio huffed a laugh and shook his head. "Get in line, sweetheart."

Sam tipped her head to the side, narrowed her eyes at him. "Listen, we're not staying. This is his lab partner, she needs to speak with him about the class. Do you know where he is?"

The three boys exchanged confused looks; the one with his hands on my hips leaned forward to my ear. "You're Sandeke's lab partner?"

I nodded, finally finding my voice. "Yes. Both semesters. It's really important that I speak to him about, um…a project we're supposed to be doing over the break. Also, I'd really appreciate it if you would remove your hands."

He blinked at me, frowned, then removed his hands and took a step back—or as much of a step back as he could manage in the crush. "You really are his lab partner?"

His eyes seemed to search my face with interest. In fact, all three of them seemed to be looking at me a little funny. I smoothed my hand down my skirt again and was thankful for the dim lights. Under their triple-handsome-perusal, I knew I was blushing uncontrollably.

"She is, she's the astronaut's daughter," the one with blue eyes finally said, as though he'd just realized and therefore, recognized me. He said it as though I were a celebrity.

This was aggravating.

I pressed my lips together before muttering, "He's my grandfather."

"I'm in Professor Gentry's class too." Blue-eyes extended his hand, captured mine; his expression was probing and tinged with respect as it moved over my face. "You look really different outside of class. Did you do something different to…your face?"

I thought about responding that I'd be happy to do something different to his face, like punch it, but Sam spoke first.

"So, can you three amigos take us to Martin?" Sam seemed to dislike this last question about my face just as much as I did, because her tone held moderate aggravation. "We don't have a lot of time."

This was a true statement. It was already 10:10 p.m. and I knew, based on my eavesdropping, that the "drugging" would occur sometime around 10:30 p.m.

Mr. Blue-eyes nodded, still holding my hand. "Sure, sure. Follow me." He tugged me forward.

Mr. Brown-eyes, the one who felt comfortable putting his hands on my body, winked at me as I passed. "Find me later, we'll have some fun."

His companion hit him on the back of the head and I heard him say as we left, "Not likely, dumbass."

"I'm Eric," Blue-eyes tossed at us over his shoulder. "Stroke is this way."

"Stroke?"

"Martin is Stroke." Eric turned briefly to explain. We made a chain, the three of us, as we wove through bodies of scantily dressed females and grabby frat boys. "He's eight seat in the boat. It's called the stroke seat because it sets the stroke rhythm for the rest of the boat. So we call him Stroke."

I gritted my teeth through the jostling, ignored the body parts that pressed against me—or outright palmed my anatomy.

Martin was called *Stroke.* Somehow that nickname fit.

Eric led us to a staircase where another bouncer dude stood. He nodded once to Eric and smirked at Sam and me. I deduced he thought we were on our way to engage in a throupling (a threesome coupling). This, of course, caused my blush to intensify.

Jerk conscience.

I struggled to climb the stairs in the heels, almost asked Eric to stop so I could remove them. I was so busy debating whether or not to take off my shoes that I almost collided with Eric's back when he stopped in front of a pair of overly large double doors.

"He's in here." Eric turned, tilted his head, then let go of my hand to push open the door.

"Thanks." I nodded once and gripped Sam's hand tighter as I moved to enter.

"No. No. She stays out here." Eric shook his head and motioned to Sam.

"What? Why?"

"Only one girl at a time, unless both are invited."

I glanced at Sam and imagined I wore a similarly stunned expression.

"Excuse me?" Sam asked. "What is he? A sultan? Does he have a harem?"

Eric smirked, his eyes moved over Sam with simmering appraisal. "I'll keep you company, cupcake."

"No thanks, dildo," she responded.

This only made his grin widen, though he said, "You're safe with me. I promise the only thing I'll do to you is stare at you."

She glowered. He narrowed his eyes mockingly, though his amusement and enjoyment at the exchange was obvious.

"I'm not worried about me," Sam explained. "I don't trust your boy around my girl, not in this house."

Eric's gaze moved over my dress; his grin waned, softened, like he knew a secret about me.

"Kaitlyn will be safe. But if she's not out in fifteen minutes we'll go rescue her together."

I didn't like what his words inferred or what they implied. I wasn't a damsel. I wasn't going to need rescuing. If anyone was a damsel in this situation it was Martin Sandeke. I was rescuing him, he just didn't know that yet...

I addressed Sam, my voice lowered. "I'll be fine. Martin's not going to do anything. I'll just tell him about the, um, the assignment and then I'll leave."

Sam was teetering, still undecided. After a prolonged moment she blurted, "Oh, all right." Then she shifted her gaze to Eric. "But I'm timing this. I have a watch." She held up her wrist so he could see the evidence of her timepiece.

"Noted," he said with a large smile, then held his hands up as though he surrendered.

Before I lost my nerve, I turned the handle to the door and opened it—only glancing back once at Sam before I stepped in and shut it behind me.

[3]
THE PERIODIC TABLE

I DON'T KNOW what I expected, but it wasn't a pool table.

I hovered at the entrance to the room, just inside the small alcove, and watched as Martin and three other guys good-naturedly knocked the cue ball around with their pool sticks.

No one noticed me at first and this allowed me time to chant my synonyms silently.

Unsteady, uncertain, nervous, anxious, worried, panic...

Then the thought popped in my mind, *Even though you don't feel calm doesn't mean you can't be calm.* This was something my mother had said often when I struggled with childhood angst, frustration, and disappointment. These words were an excellent mantra now.

I wasn't concerned for my safety, but I was concerned. I'd gone through life hiding in cabinets; I was perfectly happy to continue this practice once this task was over. I just had to get it over with first.

Propelled by this determination—to cross this task off my conscience's list and go find a nice, safe cabinet to hide in—I gained a step forward and cleared my throat.

One of the guys was mid-laugh and I wondered at first if they'd heard me. But, eventually, four sets of eyes swung to my position, though I tried to focus only on Martin.

"Uh, hi. Hello." I gave the room a little wave.

Martin, like the rest, looked at me like I was a stranger. However, I felt all pairs of eyes sweep up and down in a way that made me feel like I was a car, or a horse—one they were thinking about riding.

Heated anxiety seized my chest, tightness spread into my stomach. I balled my hands into fists and took another step into the room, further into the light.

"I'm looking for Martin." I kept my eyes on him; at six feet away, he was the closest to my position.

Recognition had not yet registered when he replied sounding both bored and irritated, "What do you want?"

"It's me. Um, it's Parker. Kaitlyn Parker. I was hoping I could speak with you for…a…minute…about chemistry?" I bit my lip, waited for his reaction.

Martin visibly stiffened, blinked, and flinched when I said my name. His eyes—now focused and narrowed—moved over me once more, this time with obvious and renewed interest.

"Parker?" He took a step forward and laid his cue stick on the table; he sounded and looked baffled.

I nodded and hazarded a glance at the others. They were alternately watching me then turning their heads to watch Martin's reaction.

"Yep. I promise I'll just be a minute, it won't take—"

"Everyone out," Martin interrupted, his voice a bit too loud for the space. It was a command.

To my surprise, his three companions set down their pool cues on the table and shuffled out as instructed, and without delay.

One or two of them caught my eye as they left, their expressions plainly curious but none of them spoke. Martin's gaze never left my face; he seemed to recover quickly from the surprise of my arrival. The line of his jaw grew hard, and the muscle at his temple ticked.

I didn't know what to make of the gathering storm in his eyes so I ignored it and attempted to think of a word to use in my synonym game. I also tried not to look at his lips.

I tried and I failed.

I couldn't help it; the memory of his kiss—our kiss—arrived like a tsunami, flooding my body with something heated and tight. I felt overwhelmed by it, surrounded on all sides. I knew what he tasted like, how he sounded when he growled, what his hands felt like on my bare skin.

I tried not to shiver and failed at that too.

The door clicked behind me, but, to me, it sounded like a gunshot —because it signaled that we were alone. I gathered a breath and tucked my hair behind my ears. I needed to focus on reciting the speech I'd practiced in my head for the last five hours.

Then I could leave, my conscience could piss off, and this would all be over.

Ignoring the goosebumps he'd ignited with his scorching glare, I did my best impression of calm and said, "So, the reason I'm here—"

"Let me guess." He crossed his broad arms over his broad chest, his broad shoulders stiff and straight, and leaned his hips, which were narrow and not broad, against the pool table. "Your level of interested has…changed."

I squinted at him. "What?"

"You've changed your mind about me." The way he said the words, deadpan and caustic, led me to the conclusion that he thought I was there to beg for more kisses, entrap him with my feminine wiles.

Little did he know, I possessed no feminine wiles. Only the willies and the heebie jeebies.

I squinted more. I was feeling flustered. He wasn't supposed to talk. He was supposed to listen.

"No. It's not that at all. It's about the cabinet."

He scoffed, like he didn't believe me. "Nice dress."

I glanced down at myself, my hand automatically lifting to my abdomen. "Uh, thanks. It's borrowed."

"Really?" He said *really* like he didn't *really* believe me.

"Yes. It's also a little too short, I think." I tugged at the hem, wishing it longer. "I was told I wouldn't be allowed in without a skirt."

His attention moved to where my hands were now fiddling with the edge of the dress and lingered there. Martin straightened from the pool table and crossed to where I stood—his steps unhurried, his gaze leisurely skating up my body. Again, I felt like a horse being perused for a ride.

"You could always take it off, the dress, if it makes you feel uncomfortable."

A full-on, fire-alarm embarrassed flush rose to my cheeks. He stopped just in front of me. His eyes were shamelessly resting on the swell of my breasts with a suggestiveness that completely crossed the appropriate line.

It was so beyond appropriate it was…

It was…

It was inappropriate.

I gathered a slow breath, hoping to steady myself, and stomped down the rising wave of indescribable sensations plaguing my sensibilities—some pleasant, some not so pleasant.

"Listen," I said through a jaw mostly clenched. "I overheard something when I was in the cabinet, before you arrived, and I thought you should know. That's the only reason I'm here."

His eyes flickered to mine, still hard, disbelieving. He was standing just a foot or so away and I'd tilted my chin upward to meet his glare.

After a pause, during which he studied my face, Martin said, "Go ahead, gorgeous. Enlighten me."

"I heard two people walk into the room. So, I panicked and, yes, I hid in the cabinet. But, in my defense, I was already in there pulling out the reticulation equipment. Anyway, two voices—one female, one male—and they came into the lab together. Whoever the guy was when you walked into the lab, that was the same guy I overheard. The girl wanted the guy to drug you."

Martin's eyebrows bounced upward then pulled low when I said the word *drug*. I didn't want him to interrupt me again so I spoke faster.

"She said she wanted him to drug you. They scheduled it for ten thirty tonight and he is supposed to make sure you stick around at the party. She said she would arrive at eleven then take you, drugged, up to your room and video tape the two of you. Then she said something truly disturbing—not that the rest of it isn't already disturbing—but what she said next kind of blew me away because I didn't know people could be that cold and calculating with no regard for basic decency."

"What did she say?" he asked, his tone impatient. His eyes were still hard, angry, but the severity wasn't focused on me. I didn't appear to be the target—praise Bunsen and his burner!

"She said that if she got pregnant then it would be 'a bonus.'"

Martin's mouth opened then closed and his glare moved from me to the floor. He was visibly stunned. I watched his beautiful face as he processed the information, took the opportunity to examine him in a way I'd never allowed myself to do before.

He was painfully handsome. I kind of knew that before, but I really saw it now.

My chest hurt a little as I studied his features: square jaw, strong nose, perfect shape and size for his face, high cheekbones, like he had Cherokee or Navaho ancestry. Paired with his blue eyes, he was striking. I understood my previous reluctance to gaze at him directly. It was called self-preservation.

I tore my eyes from him and his exceptional form. I tried not to notice his decidedly swoony body—the way his jeans hung on his hips, the way his thighs filled out the jeans—and glanced over his shoulder.

"Well. That was what I needed to tell you. So, I guess I'll be—"

"Why should I trust you?"

My eyes moved back to his and I blinked at this question, because the answer was obvious. "Uh, what?"

"How do I know you're telling me the truth?"

"Why would I lie?"

"What do you expect in exchange?"

"Exchange for what?"

He shifted on his feet just a fraction of an inch closer. However, that fraction brought with it a menacing cloud of suspicion and unpleasantness.

For someone so beautiful, his expression was surprisingly ugly.

"What is it that you want? What are you hoping to gain? Is it money?"

My mouth fell open and my nose wrinkled again, this time in outrage. I looked at him, really looked at him—and this time I wasn't seeing the outer façade of blinding beauty. What I saw was a guy who was bitter, jaded, and maybe a little desperate—for what, I had no idea.

Finally I said, "What is wrong with you?"

His eyebrows shot up. "What's wrong with me?"

"Yes," I countered, my hands coming to my hips. "What is wrong with you? I came here to *help* you, the least you could do is not act like a jerk-face."

"Jerk-face?" he shot back, his eyes growing both hot and cold. "You show up here, looking like that, and you expect me to believe you're not after something?"

"I already told you, jerk-face, it's a skirt party! I wouldn't have made it through the door if I hadn't been wearing this stupid dress, jerk-face. If you don't like how I look, jerk-face, then you can go yell at your stupid sorority brothers."

"You mean fraternity brothers."

"Sorority, sorostitute, fraternity, fratigalo—whatever! It's all the same to me."

"So I'm supposed to believe that you have no ulterior motive? If this is true then why didn't you tell me all of this at the lab?" He gained another half step forward and, since I refused to back down, only inches separated us.

"Because you scratched my itch and then you kissed me—both of which freaked me out because neither of which are in the course syllabus for laboratory experiments this semester. And, furthermore—"

I didn't get to finish because the door opened behind me and a voice I recognized called into the room. "Hey Stroke—dude, why are you up here? I brought you a drink. Some of my special hunch punch."

I'd turned toward the sound of the voice and stumbled a step backward. Martin's arm wrapped around my shoulders, bringing my shoulders to his chest as the owner of the voice leaned halfway in—two red solo cups extended.

The guy, about two inches taller than Martin—therefore, very tall —walked through the door after a short pause. Behind him I could see Eric standing with Sam. They both peered into the room and I noted Eric's face was apologetic as he glanced at Martin.

I tried to step forward but Martin's arm tightened, held me still.

The stranger's clear blue eyes moved from me to Martin, then back again. "Hey—Eric said you had company so I brought one for both of you."

I knew his voice because it was *him*. The cuss monster from the lab.

I felt Martin's chest expand on a slow inhale, his fingers were digging into my arm; it wasn't painful but it was pointed, firm, meant to communicate a message—*don't move*.

"Thanks, Ben," Martin drawled, but the edge in his voice was glacial and he made no move to accept the cups.

Ben gave me a stiff smile, his eyes lingering on where Martin's arm was wrapped around me, then he raised both cups. "You two should have a toast. Come down to the party."

"Leave the drinks and go," Martin said.

Ben frowned, glanced at the two cups and cleared his throat. "You should come downstairs, this is epic—"

"Go," Martin repeated.

This time Ben nodded once and set the cups on a table by the door. "Sure, sure. I'll come back in a bit to see if you need any more." He held his hands up and backed out of the room, his eyes completing another once over of my body before he closed the door.

I exhaled the breath I'd been holding and, just for a moment, allowed myself to lean against Martin.

"That was him. That was the guy—I recognize his voice."

I felt Martin nod, his chin and cheek against the side of my hair. We stood—still, quiet—for a long moment, then he turned me to face him. Both of his hands moved to my waist and he backed me against the pool table.

His eyes, guarded, but also tempered with curiosity, searched mine. I still saw desperation in his features and it still perplexed me. I didn't touch him. Instead I braced my hands on either side of my hips where my body met the pool table.

At length he asked, "What do you want?"

I swallowed then responded, "I'd like to leave."

He shook his head slowly. "That's not what I meant. What do you want from me?"

I shrugged. "It would be great if you could tabulate the findings from last week's assignment, but I'm not going to hold my breath." He never did the tabulations and analyses. It was annoying.

"Parker."

"What?"

His eyes dipped to my mouth and his voice was the softest I'd ever heard it, almost coaxing. "Kaitlyn…"

I stiffened against the feelings associated with my name from his lips, spoken in gentle tones.

I averted my eyes and my voice was a little strained when I said, "Martin, I honestly don't want anything from you. I'd like to leave so I can change into my normal clothes, drink tea, eat cookies, and read a good book in my dorm room."

"Kaitlyn, look at me."

Once again, my neck flushed and my arms broke out in goosebumps.

I tried to ignore both the blush and the goosebumps. "I also want for you to forget any of this happened so that we can go back to being lab partners."

He was quiet for a long time, but I knew—even though I refused to meet his gaze—that he was studying me, examining me like I was something new.

Then he said, "Why do you hide?"

The words startled me so much that my eyes instinctively sought his, and this was a mistake. His gaze—now a lovely blue fire—was taking a survey of my face, as though he were memorizing every detail. It was alarming and my heart quickened.

I tried for a shrug but it likely looked like a poorly executed, convulsive shiver. "Why do you care?"

His gaze met mine then flickered to my lips. "You have fantastic lips."

I half choked, my eyes widening. "You care because I have fantastic lips?"

"And your eyes. They're grey. I noticed them first." His voice was just above a whisper; he sounded as though he was talking to himself.

I cleared my throat, not really sure what to say. But it turned out I didn't need to say anything, because he continued.

"Early last semester you wore a tank top and your hair was down. You kept pulling it off your neck." He lifted his hand and brushed the backs of his fingers against my swell of cleavage, skirting the neckline of the dress, a soft caress. "I tried to get your phone number but you wouldn't give it to me."

"I give out my number as rarely as possible, it's one of my life rules," I said dumbly.

"The red pants, the tight ones that show off your ass. You tortured me, bending over to get supplies out of the cabinet. That isn't very nice."

My voice was unaccountably breathless. "The corduroy ones? I only wear those when all my other laundry is dirty."

"You're better at chemistry than me, you ace all the tests."

"I like chemistry, and you don't study like you should."

"Haven't you ever wondered why I come on Fridays?" His fingers curled around my neck and his thumb traced circles along the line of my collarbone. He encouraged my head to tip backward.

"So that we can get a jump start on the weekly assignment?"

He shook his head. "You."

My eyelashes fluttered. "Me?"

His held me captive with both his heavily lidded gaze and his caressing hands. Martin leaned forward, and he brushed his lips against mine. It wasn't a kiss. It was more like he was using his lips to feel mine, to enjoy my softness.

"You," he whispered again.

My fingers gripped the wood on either side of my hips and I

successfully fought a whimper. The tightness in my chest eased and twisted, my stomach fluttered, my breath coming shallow and fast.

My brain wasn't quite working properly because he'd muddled it—with his words, hands, and lips of temptation. Therefore, in a paltry attempt to defend myself from his seduction onslaught, I blurted out one of my greatest fears where he was concerned.

"You'll make me cry."

His eyes widened a little, moved between mine. "I wouldn't."

"You would. I've seen it, I see how you treat girls."

His hand at my waist tightened. "I wouldn't do that to you. You're not...I know you're not like that. We wouldn't be that."

"I don't trust you."

He sighed, but not with impatience. "I know." He nodded. "But you will."

He dipped his head again, placed a soft kiss on my lips, just a hint of his tongue. It wasn't enough. My hands lifted on their own and gripped his shirt, staying any retreat he might have planned. I didn't do this on purpose. In fact, I didn't know why I did it.

"Martin, I can't—"

"You can."

"I'm not—"

"You are."

"You don't—"

"I do." He kissed me again and shifted his weight more completely against me. Martin crowded my space so that he filled every inch of it. Four of my senses were overwhelmed by him—the smell of his cologne, his hot and hard body against mine, the taste of his mouth, the low growl in the back of his throat when our tongues met and mated.

Briefly he drew his mouth from mine, and demanded, "Say you'll spend the week with me."

I blinked, started to protest. "Martin, this isn't—"

He kissed me again, placed my arms around his neck, then his hands moved up my ribs and his palm cupped me through the thin material of my dress. His thumb drew tight circles around the center of my breast.

He growled, "Say it. Spend the week with me."

I moaned, because…aroused.

He bit my lip, sucked it between his. I moaned again.

"You're so fucking beautiful, Kaitlyn." He breathed the words suddenly, like he didn't mean to say them out loud, but they burst forth unbidden. "I want you to spend the week with me. Say yes."

He kissed me again, quickly, then trailed wet, hot kisses over my jaw and behind my ear to my shoulder. He bit me—hard—and sucked on my neck in a way that made me squirm and my breath hitch; all the while his large hand massaged my breast and tortured me through the fabric. His other hand had moved to my bottom and pressed my center to his.

"Martin…" was all I could manage, because…*really* aroused. And, not that I was an expert, but judging by the hard length against my stomach, he was also really aroused.

"Please, say yes," he breathed into my ear.

I said, "Yes…"

"Promise me."

"I promise."

To be honest, I said it but I didn't mean it. In that moment, I said yes because he'd asked me to—and he'd used the word *please* and I didn't want all the good feelings to stop—not because I had any intention of spending the week with Martin Sandeke, Hercules, jerk to women, and apparently king of seducing naïve and intimacy-starved virgins.

Regardless, my words seemed to be enough for Martin because he smiled against my skin and stopped talking. He also moved both of his hands from their shockingly effective ministrations and encircled me in his arms. His mouth moved back to mine.

This time the kiss was slow, less urgent, gentle, and sweet. It felt like a prelude, a beginning. When he lifted his head, I opened my eyelids to find him gazing down at me, his eyes alight—blue flames.

"I'll pick you up tomorrow," he said. His voice was different, softer, deeper…content.

"What?" I blinked at him.

"Be ready at eight."

"Eight?"

"You don't need to pack much." He kissed my nose, released me from his arms, threaded his fingers through mine, and tugged me toward the door. "I hope you like private beaches."

[4]
ENTHALPIES OF REACTION

"**W**HAT ARE YOU going to do?"

"Nothing."

I heard Sam shift in her seat causing the leather to creak. "What do you mean *nothing*? He's expecting you to go away with him for spring break."

I shrugged, staring out the window of Martin's chauffeured car. That's right. A *chauffeured* car, for a twenty-year-old college student. If I hadn't felt so pensive I might've looked for the Grey Poupon Dijon mustard.

After my lapse in judgment against the pool table, Martin had navigated Sam and me to the back of the fraternity house while calling his driver on the phone. The man was at the back door by the time we arrived.

Martin pulled me in for a quick kiss—which was completely bizarre, provocative, and off-putting—then unceremoniously loaded us in, telling his driver to take us to our dorm.

Sam pumped me for information as soon as the door shut. I related the facts, which gave me an opportunity to recover a measure of sanity. In hindsight, I realized I'd been acting like a crazy person. Proximity to

Martin made me lose my sense. I'd been senseless. Without sense. Not any sense. No sense.

Nonsense.

I spoke to the window rather than be faced with Sam's anxious expression. "I mean, I'm going to do nothing. I can't be held responsible for my reactions—what I say or what I do—when faced with a real life Martin Sandeke. He's the man equivalent of a gun to the head, except without the fear for my life aspect. I'll write him an email, tell him that he adversely affects my ability to function as a rational being. As such, our discussion this evening and all resultant agreements are null and void. I'm sure he'll understand."

I felt like I had stumbled into an alternate reality and was just now finding my way out of the rabbit hole.

Sam snorted. "Um, no. He's not going to understand. And, I doubt he'll take no for an answer. He's kind of a bully that way, or least he has that reputation."

This statement captured my curiosity; I turned in my seat to face Sam. "Wait, what do you mean? Does he—has he forced himself on—"

"No! God, no. I would never have teased you about getting his number if he forced himself on girls. That's not what I meant. He wouldn't need to do that in any case, as he has them lined up around the fraternity house with skirts up to their elbows, willing to bend whichever direction he prefers. I bet that's why he was hiding upstairs. It must get exhausting at some point..." Sam trailed off and I got the sense she was speaking mostly to herself.

I frowned at Sam. "Rape isn't about need, it's about power."

"Exactly. Sorry if I implied otherwise. Regardless, Martin Sandeke has a reputation for getting it on with a cornucopia of willing females."

"Then what are you talking about? How is he a bully? Other than making females he's slept with cry and getting into fist fights." I listened to the words as they left my mouth, realizing that those two facts made him enough of a bully to be labeled as such.

"I just mean he's used to getting his way, right? He has his own yacht. His. Own. Yacht." She stared at me, her eyebrows raised with meaning. "If he wants something, it's his. He doesn't even ask, he just mentions it."

I twisted my lips to the side and considered this information, not really understanding why it was pertinent to our discussion. "So? What has that got to do with me?"

Sam's eyelids drooped with disbelief, but her eyebrows stayed suspended. "Have you not been paying attention? I saw the way he looked at you, the way he held your hand all the way to the car, the way he kissed you before we left. He wants you. Martin Sandeke wants you."

I considered her, her words, and sighed. "I'm not a yacht."

"No. You're a girl. He's had hundreds of girls. But he has only one yacht." Then under her breath she added, "Well, he has only one yacht that I know of."

"Sam, weren't you the one pushing me to get his number?"

"Yes, but that was before I was told to stand outside while you went into his lair. That was before I saw the dazed look on your face when you emerged from the aforementioned lair. That was before I found out he wants you to go away with him for a week! I want you to get your freak on, but I don't want you to get your heart broken."

"I think you're overreacting. You said yourself, he has them lined up around the block. I'll politely decline his offer, and he'll move on to someone else. There is no need to become hysterical."

"I'm not hysterical and you are being purposefully obtuse."

"Fine. I'll sleep with him. I'll call him tomorrow and tell him I want to get it over with. Then, by your logic, he'll go away. Problem solved."

Sam growled. "That's not a good idea either."

"Well, what do you want me to do?"

"You should tell him face-to-face that you don't want to go. You should explain your reasons why and establish boundaries for future interactions. And you should have me there as your representative to make sure he doesn't try to zap you with his sexy ray."

"Zap me with his sexy ray?"

"You know what I'm talking about. I barely saw him and I'm

feeling the effects. He's got like an…electromagnetic pulse of sexy or something. So does his friend, Eric. They're a menace. They shouldn't be allowed in public."

"That's not how electromagnets work."

"Whatever. You get my point."

"We're here." The driver's voice over the speaker interrupted our conversation and drew our attention to the view of our dorm outside my window.

I heard the sound of him exiting the car, presumably walking around to open my door.

Sam covered my hand with hers bringing my attention back to her. "Just think about what I said. Carter did a number on you, but his intentions weren't hurtful. This guy," she paused, her eyes moving between mine, "if Carter was a stick of dynamite, this guy is a nuclear weapon."

* * *

THE CAMPUS EMAIL directory was public information within the school's Black Board system. I could find any person's email address by conducting a simple first name, last name, year enrolled search. However, since it was so easy to find a person's email address, very few people actually used their on-campus email account, preferring Gmail or another alternative where spam wasn't such an issue.

I knew this. I knew the chances of Martin actually receiving my email were minute. Regardless, I reasoned I would have the moral high ground if I sent him an email as soon as I arrived home. Then, when he showed up the next day and I was missing, I could point out later that I did—in fact—send him an email.

It wasn't my fault if he didn't check his email.

Martin,

I hope you are well.

I appreciate your offer to accompany you on your travels during spring break, but I've reconsidered my response. Upon gaining distance from the situation, I see that I made an error when I agreed to go with you. I simply have too much school work to do this week. As well, I volunteer at a women's crisis center as their resident desktop support. I do not want to leave without giving them proper notice as they count on me to be here when issues arise. Therefore, please accept my apologies. I'm sure you'll have no problem finding an alternative.

As well, I would appreciate it if our future topics of conversation were limited to chemistry (and only chemistry) from now on. See you in the lab.

-Parker

"What are you doing?" Sam asked as she walked into our room.

When we arrived back to the dorm, I'd gone to the bathroom first to wash my face and brush my teeth while Sam changed. Then, she went to the bathroom while I changed. But instead of changing, I pulled out my laptop.

"Nothing."

She *tsked,* putting away her toiletries. "You're sending him an email. That's a mistake."

"It doesn't matter if he gets it. I sent it. That's what matters."

"That's not what I meant. You're giving him a heads-up. Now he'll be able to plan a counter attack."

I glanced at her from the corner of my eye. "Counter attack? This is not some exercise from Sun Tsu's *The Art of War*, this is me rejecting his free vacation offer. What can he do?"

"You'll see." She said this in a sing-song voice, switching off the light on her side of the room, and climbing into bed.

"Besides. I sent it to his school account. He probably won't even get it."

"Then he'll show up tomorrow and you'll have to deal with him in person."

"No. I'll be gone. He said he'd be here at eight. I'll leave at seven and stay at the library all day."

"Coward."

"Is a chameleon a coward because it can change its color? No. It's evolved and awesome. I like to think of myself in a similar fashion.

There is nothing wrong with having a strong sense of self-preservation."

"Whatever. Do you want me to wake you up? I have tennis practice at six."

"Nah, I'll set the alarm on my phone." I closed my laptop and tucked it next to our shared nightstand, then stood to dress for bed.

After changing, I grabbed my phone to set my alarm for 6:30 a.m. I wanted to be gone long before Martin or one of his people arrived. I usually woke up around 7:30 a.m., therefore the alarm was necessary.

Upon glancing at the screen of my cell, I noticed I had two missed calls from my mother plus a text message. It read,

Just got home. Call when you can. I'll be up until 2.

My mother: senator, workaholic, efficient conversationalist, superhero.

Distracted by the message, I abandoned my alarm for the moment and dialed my mother's number. It wouldn't take long. Our discussions rarely lasted over three minutes. She answered after one point five rings.

"Kaitlyn. You have not communicated your plans for spring break. Is it your intention to join us in Monterey or are you remaining on campus?" my mother's brisk, businesslike voice sounded from the other end.

She had an agenda and talking points for every conversation. Growing up, she would hand me a paper copy and ask me to follow along. When I was very young, she used pictures in place of words and we'd discuss things like: *Three month review: Preschool. Scheduled: Haircut. Action plan required: Cleaning your room. Music: Interfering with scheduled playtime.*

Before I left for college, if one or both of my parents were traveling, the family meeting would be conducted via conference call. Now we typically held the meeting via conference call due to my physical absence from home. Topics for discussion ran the gamut of *Purchase Request: New Bike,* to *Family News: Your Grandmother has cancer,* to *Point of Concern: Time spent on music surpassing time spent on home-*

work, to *Scheduled Recreation: Yearly vacation options,* to *Kaitlyn News: Accepted to Harvard, Yale, Princeton, MIT, Caltech.*

"I am remaining on campus."

"Will Sam be present?"

"Yes."

"Do you require any funds?"

"No."

"Are you amenable to a visit with your father and me next Sunday? Brunch or lunch, Kartwell's Deli."

"Yes. Sunday. Brunch."

Even now, family meetings occurred on Sundays. My father and I would submit agenda items to George, my mother's PA (Personal Assistant) no later than Friday night. A draft agenda would be circulated Saturday afternoon for comment and the final version distributed Saturday evening. Attached to the agenda would be a copy of our individual calendars for the next month, updated weekly.

I'd fallen out of the habit of updating my calendar since leaving home. Agendas, schedules, and lists ensured we made the most efficient use of our time. I knew this. But my schedule only changed once a semester. My life was predictable, therefore I saw no need to send weekly updates.

"How is school?"

"Very well. How is work?"

To my surprise, she didn't provide her typical rapid-fire response of, "It is what it is." Instead, she paused then sighed and said, "Terrible."

My mouth opened and closed, I could feel my eyebrows jump on my forehead. "Uh…care to elaborate?"

"My Net Neutrality measure is not progressing to my satisfaction in The House, the Telecommunications lobbyists are growing rabid, and the FCC is being difficult. I am frustrated."

I immediately responded, "Net Neutrality is an important issue and worth the effort and frustration. You are doing the right thing." Every once in a while I served as my mother's cheerleader. Every so often she served as mine. These occasions were rare as we both believed in self-sufficiency unless circumstances were dire.

However, we loved each other. Neither of us were so austere as to withhold support when it was requested, but I appreciated and subscribed to her no-drama mantra. Energy should be spent on solutions to real problems—like the abysmal status of the US foster care system, or our strained foreign policy with Pakistan, or Telecommunications giants using Net Neutrality as a weapon against the public good —therefore, when she said she was frustrated it usually meant she was at her wit's end.

"Thank you. I appreciate your words of encouragement and I value your opinion." Her tone was softer. It was the voice she'd used when I was a kid and she'd read me the first three Harry Potter books before bedtime.

"Anytime."

She then surprised me further by saying, "You know I love you, right?"

Again, my mouth did its little opening and closing dance before I blurted, "Of course. Of course I know you love me. I love you too."

"Good...good."

She told me every Sunday that she loved me. It was the last thing my parents and I would exchange on our conference calls even though it wasn't listed on the agenda. A mid-week *I love you* hadn't occurred since my parents dropped me off at University my freshman year.

I was about to push her for more details on the source of her stress, because she was obviously out of sorts and had me concerned, but before I could, her efficient tone was back.

"Please send George your updated calendar with a weekly update for the period of spring break. You do not have classes next week, as such the calendar is incorrect."

"I will."

"Thank you. Goodnight, Kaitlyn."

"Goodnight, Mom."

She clicked off first. I held the phone to my ear for several seconds before lowering it to the nightstand, then distractedly readied myself for bed.

My mom was the daughter of a physicist (my grandmother) and an astronaut (my grandfather). My grandfather was also a physicist in the Navy. She'd been an overachiever her whole life and believed in goal-focused structure. She was a superhero. She was *my* hero. Therefore, moments when she allowed herself to display vulnerability were distressing. It was like watching Superman struggle through a bout of kryptonite exposure.

I returned to my pillow and comforter, both of which I loved; they smelled like lavender, and were so cozy, poems should be written about their epic cozy wonder. I snuggled against their softness and willed away the touch of anxiety I felt about my mom's strange behavior.

Eventually I fell asleep.

[5]
BASIC CONCEPTS OF CHEMICAL BONDING

"PARKER."

Fingers were in my hair, brushing it away from my face. Then the fingers caressed a path over my shoulder, down my arm, and fit themselves around mine, squeezing.

"Parker... Time to get up. Time to go." A mystery male voice reverberated in my head. It was a nice voice. It made my insides feel like a warm marshmallow, sweet and fluffy and melting.

I lifted my eyebrows but couldn't quite open my eyes; I asked in a sleep mumble, "Where are we going?"

"We're going to the beach."

The words sounded faraway and my drowsy brain told me to ignore them. I began to drift.

"You're cute when you don't want to wake up." The mystery voice sounded both growly and amused. I liked the mystery voice.

I also liked the word *cute,* but not as much as its alternates. "Adorable, captivating, charming, darling..."

"What?"

"Synonyms."

"Okay. Come on, Cutie pie. Wake up." The hand was on my face, cupping my cheek. I noted that it felt exceptionally callused. A thumb brushed back and forth, whisper light touches over my bottom lip, sending little shivers down my neck to my spine.

I opened one eye, managed a squint at the fuzzy form, and recognized the owner of the mystery voice. It was Martin Sandeke. And it looked like he was sitting on my bed. I couldn't quite make sense of it.

"What's going on?" I rubbed my eyes with the base of my palms, still someplace between my dreams and reality, but closer to dreams.

This was a dream. I was certain. It was a dream within a dream or one of those dreams that felt eerily real. Maybe, if I was lucky, I'd be able to control the action of the dream and spend some naked time with Martin Sandeke's superior physique without the danger of his personality ruining things.

"I'm picking you up for our trip." His hand settled on my bare thigh. The weight of it felt very real.

I stopped mid-eye rub, opting for motionless contemplation instead of a gasping shriek.

"Martin?" I asked to what I hoped would be an empty room.

"Yes?"

I jumped to a sitting position, my eyes flying open. "Oh my God, what are you doing here?"

Martin was sitting on the edge of my bed toward the middle. I stared at him; he was wearing dark, faded jeans, a white T-shirt, and a smile. He was so handsome I felt like filing a civil lawsuit against his parents, claiming punitive damages, pain and suffering to my psyche.

"I'm picking you up."

I reached for my phone to check the time. It was 7:00 a.m.

"What? What? Why? What?" was all I could manage, because my alarm didn't go off.

I had fallen off to sleep, but forgot to set my alarm... Gah!

So, Martin was one hour early and he was here. In my room. Sitting on my bed. Watching me like he wanted me for…things.

He leaned forward, his gaze on my mouth somehow both gentle and wicked. Horrified that he might try to kiss me first thing in the morning, I scrambled to my feet and ran off the bed, jumping from the mattress like it was a spring board. I'm sure I jostled him on my way.

I reached for my bag and pulled out my Wintermint gum, unwrapping three pieces, and shoving them into my mouth.

"It's seven," I said sloppily around the wad in my mouth.

"Yes. I'm early."

I glanced over my shoulder and found Martin Sandeke had stretched himself out on my bed, ankles crossed, leaning against my pillow, his laced together fingers resting behind his head.

Turning fully around, I aggressively chewed and stared at him. His eyes were moving up and down my body with a heated and slow appraisal. I glanced down at myself. I was wearing my Sponge Bob Square Pants tank top and sleep shorts. But I wasn't wearing a bra and my shape was easily discernable through the fitted shirt.

I crossed my arms over my chest and stiffened my spine. "How did you get in?"

"I have my ways…" He'd gone from appraising to ogling. He licked his lips. The action felt malicious. "Why don't you come over here?"

"I'm perfectly fine over here," I said primly, but the effect was ruined by the gob of gum in my mouth that was quickly losing its flavor. I reached for a napkin next to my food stuffs and daintily rid myself of the gum, tossing it into the trash two feet from my position. The nice thing about dorms is that everything is within reach.

However, I'd positioned myself on the side opposite the door. If I wanted to leave I'd have to walk by Martin on my way out.

Abruptly he said, "Bring the red pants."

"What?"

"When you pack, bring those red pants. I've been thinking about them a lot."

I sputtered, "I'm not bringing the red pants."

He shrugged, his hands still folded behind his head. "Fine. Don't bring the red pants. Bring nothing."

"I'm not bringing nothing, I'm not bringing anything!"

"Good. We're in agreement."

"That's not what I meant. I'm not bringing anything because I'm not going."

He squinted at me. "You promised."

"Under duress."

"I wasn't holding a gun to your head."

"No, just holding yourself to my body. That's quite enough to put me in a state of duress."

"My body places you in a state of duress?" Something wicked sparked behind his eyes.

"Of course. Of course it does. What a ridiculous question. Your body causes distress, disquiet, desolation, and puts me in a state of duress."

He grinned, sitting up in the bed like he planned to stand up. "Maybe I'll use it now."

"Please don't." I held up my hand as though it could stop him. It didn't stop him. He stood, reached for and closed the door, then whipped his shirt off. My mouth went dry. My heart thumped painfully. My girl parts forcefully made their opinion known.

Me want Martin flavored cookie! Me want cookie now!!

The sight was indecent because the sight immediately made me want to do several indecent things to him, around him, near him, on top, underneath, adjacent to—if it was a preposition, I wanted to do it with Martin.

"Ack! No!" I squeezed my eyes shut and covered my face with my hands. "Not the chest! Anything but the chest!"

"Anything?" I did not miss the wicked teasing in his taunt, nor did I miss the distinct sound of a zipper being undone.

"Okay, I lied. Shirtless is fine, just please, please, please don't take off your pants." I turned from him, still covering my face with one hand, and blindly reached for the door of the closet with the other. The closet ran the length of one wall and had sliding doors. I knew I would be able to fit inside. Maybe I could barricade myself until he left, or throw my shoes at him like missiles.

For the first time in my life I wished I owned spiky heels instead of mostly sneakers. I did have one pair of Doc Martins, however…

His pants hit the floor, the change in his pocket jingling on the descent, and I imagined he was now toeing off his shoes.

"For the love of Bunsen, please put your pants back on." My voice sounded desperate because I was desperate.

I slid the closet door open just as Martin's hands claimed my hips from behind. I stiffened because he pressed his bare chest to my back and his groin to my bottom. He was hard and I was soft, and I was convinced I was about to die of… something related to abrupt sexual desire. I released a tortured moan because I could feel his stiff thickness through his boxers—or briefs, or boxer briefs.

Unthinkingly I reached around me, my eyes still shut, and encountered the thin cotton of his boxer briefs just as he bit and kissed my neck. I yanked my hand back. "You're in your underwear."

"So are you."

"Oh my God. Who does that? Why would you do that?"

"I'm launching a counter attack."

"A counter attack? I haven't attacked. You can't launch a counter attack until the other person has attacked."

"Fine." Kiss. Bite. Tongue. Lick. "Then it's a preemptive strike," he said, hand under my shirt, on my stomach. Other hand over my shirt, kneading my breast.

Some instinct had me pressing my bottom backward and against him as I arched into the hand toying with my breast.

"You think I'm only interested in you for one thing. You're wrong," he whispered against my ear, hot breath spilling against my neck making me shiver, his hand on my stomach inching lower.

"This, what you're doing now, how you're touching me, does not give credibility to your words." My breath hitched, my brain disengaging.

"You're wrong. I'll prove it to you."

"I'm right. I'm right. I'm so, so, so right." I sighed, my hands abandoning the closet door and reaching behind me to touch his body. My center ached. My stomach fluttered. My skin was on fire. Lust and madness had descended.

"You're coming with me. There is nothing temporary about how I want you." His thumb was tracing a circle around my nipple. He pinched it roughly, causing me to suck in a startled—yet delighted —breath.

He was so talented at this. So very, very skillful. His movements were expert, practiced. Meanwhile, I was fumbling, a creature of instinct, reacting to his proficient petting.

"Do you like this?" he asked, his voice sounding dark and lovely against the shell of my ear. "Does it feel good?"

I nodded.

"Do you want more? Say yes or no."

"Yes," I gasped. "So much yes."

The fingers of his other hand delved into my panties, his long middle finger stroking my center. If I hadn't been lost to lust and madness, I would definitely have been embarrassed by the state of my nether region.

I was sure the girls he was used to had porn-star vaginas—waxed, smooth, bleached for color tone consistency, surgically enhanced to make them appear less like a forest floor—but I was au naturel down-stairs. I'd never had a reason to do anything beyond trimming the hedge for hygiene's sake.

But I wasn't embarrassed. I was a little terrified and a lot confused, but mostly I was trapped in Martin's erotic haze. I was bucking against him because his finger had just entered me.

"Whoa!" I panted.

"Fuck," he breathed against the back of my neck, his teeth sharp as they bit my spine. "You are so tight. So fucking tight."

"That's because I'm a virgin and I'm aroused," I said unthinkingly on an exhale. "The vaginal canal swells when aroused."

His hands stilled—both at my breast and in my panties—though his penis seemed to push more insistently against my ass, as though raising its head and saying, *Tell me more about this vaginal canal swelling of which you speak.*

"What?" he asked, his tone sharp, exacting.

"It's true, it swells." I shifted restlessly when he remained motion-less. "It also elongates."

"You're a virgin?"

It was my turn to hold still, a spike of some unpleasant sensation coursing through my body. I hadn't meant to admit that. I hadn't meant to ever tell him anything personal about myself, anything that could be tucked away and used to make me cry at some later date.

"Um…," I said, struggling to think of some way to hide that fact without flat-out lying.

Martin withdrew his hands and I felt the loss of him at my back; a few seconds later I heard the jingle of the change in his pants pocket. I closed my eyes again, my forehead hitting the closet door.

"Ah, barnacles," I whispered, my body cold and hot. I was tightly wound with both mortification and unspent sexual energy.

"You're a virgin," he said, this time not a question; it sounded like an accusation.

I nodded, took a deep breath, and glanced over my shoulder. He was buttoning his jeans, his expression thunderous. I glared at where his fingers gripped the waist of his pants.

"So what?" I said. If I pretended like it was no big deal maybe he'd believe me. "So what, I'm a virgin."

Finished with his button, he pulled the zipper up with a rough yank. "So you're a virgin and I'm not going to—" He growled, cutting himself off and reached for his shirt with a rough swipe. "I'm not a total bastard," he said, this to his shirt.

I glared at him, disbelieving what he'd just said, what he'd just implied. "What does my being a virgin have to do with anything? All girls should be treated with respect regardless of whether or not they're virgins. Being a virgin doesn't make me any more or less worthwhile than a non-virgin. Your seduction logic is flawed."

"It's not virgins I have a problem with. I've fucked plenty of virgins."

I winced at this and watched him pull his shirt on with jerky movements. Before I could recover from his harsh admission, he continued.

"But you being a virgin and you being Kaitlyn Parker makes me want to ensure our first time touching each other isn't some grope session against the closet of a dorm room."

"So if I hadn't been a virgin, then we would…what? We would

have just, just…" I couldn't say the word *fuck*. I just couldn't. Instead I rushed to finish. "You would have impaled me with your penis while I face planted against the closet?"

"God, Kaitlyn. No!" His protest appeared to be equally appalled and earnest. "I wanted to tease you until you agreed to come with me. I wasn't going to let it go that far. Haven't you ever fooled around before?"

I think he knew the answer before he finished asking the question, because his eyes widened with realization as the last words left his mouth.

No. No, I have never fooled around.

I didn't want to admit anything. Yet I couldn't help but look away, stare unseeingly at the foot of my bed. I belatedly realized my small evasive action told him everything. My hands balled into fists and I crossed my arms over my chest. The weight and heat of his gaze, what he must be thinking about me, made my skin feel three sizes too small.

"Damnit, Kaitlyn! Was I your first kiss too?" He sounded angry and his words made me jump.

"No. Of course not." My cheeks and neck were on fire. I tried to lift my eyes to his but couldn't manage any higher than his chin. "I've kissed someone before."

"*Someone*? As in, one other person?"

For some inexplicable reason, I felt like crying. Tears stung behind my eyelids and my throat felt tight.

I knew it.

I KNEW IT.

I knew he was going to make me cry. It's what he did. Therefore, I didn't answer him. I just blinked at the foot of my bed and pressed my lips together, focused on my breathing.

He sat down heavily on the edge of my bed, his elbows on his knees, running his hands through his hair, and I heard him exhale a dumbfounded, "Fuck."

I muttered, "That word is unimaginative."

"You're completely inexperienced." He said this to the room.

He was probably thinking, *What is wrong with you that you've only been kissed by one other person? That you never made it past first base prior to yesterday?*

"I've read books," I said dumbly, clearing my throat, safely past the threat of tears. "And watched a number of pornographic videos. I took extensive notes. I've also read several enlightening journal articles on pubmed about the physiology of the sex act. I probably know more about the logistics of it then you do. I'm not an idiot."

"No. *You're* not the idiot," he said. Again, he sounded angry. He bent to put on his shoes and I noted that his jaw flexed, and he was grinding his teeth.

I shifted uncomfortably on my feet. The instinct to hide was strong. I considered stepping backward into the closet and sliding the door shut. Maybe he wouldn't notice. He'd just look up eventually and it would look like I'd simply disappeared.

I was about to put this plan into action when he stood abruptly. It startled me so I did a weird step forward then backward shuffle, similar to a jazz square. He crossed to me, his eyes fierce, his gaze intent. I retreated until my back hit the closet, lifting my chin to maintain eye contact.

"This is what is going to happen," he said, his hands moving like he was going to touch me, but then he yanked them back at the last minute and stuffed them in his pockets. "Pack your things, you're coming with me."

I opened my mouth to protest, but he cut me off.

"You promised, Parker. You said yes and you promised."

Not breaking promises was one of my life rules. If I made a promise, I kept it. Therefore I frowned at him and admitted nothing.

He studied me for a moment, his gaze growing thoughtful, introspective. His words sounded shaded with distraction as he said, "We're going to take this slow. We're going to start over and do this right."

I squinted at him, my mouth doing its opening and closing dance. "What? What are you talking about? Take what slow?"

"You like me." He said this matter-of-factly, with a hint of belligerence.

This statement did not answer my question.

"What?"

"You like me. You want to know me better."

"I most certainly do not want to know you better."

"I definitely want to know you better." His gaze flickered down then up meaningfully.

I gaped at him because—hot hottie from Hotsvillie—the growly and intense way he'd said, *I definitely want to know you better* made my insides flare into a frenzy of wanting that *wanted* him to know me better.

My immediate thought was, *Okay, let's do that. Let's just do whatever you want, just say everything using that voice, mmm-kay?*

He continued, "We'll have dates."

Because my mind was distracted, I didn't understand his meaning, therefore I said, "I don't like dates. They're too sugary and stick to my teeth."

His somber and fierce façade cracked, a small smile tugging at the side of his mouth. He leaned closer, resting his hand on the closet behind me, his face just inches from mine.

His truly magnificent eyes were bright with amusement and something else as they scanned my face. His truly magnificent lips formed a mesmerizing curve. His truly magnificent body was scant inches from mine, but touched me nowhere.

"Fine." His voice was quiet and laced heavily with intimacy. "We won't have dates on our dates. We'll have tacos."

"I like tacos." I said this because I did like tacos, but I was also mesmerized by the voodoo of his closeness.

"Good. Tacos. Promise me." He stuck out his hand.

"I promise." I took his hand, shook it, released it, then frowned. "Wait, what?"

His eyes darted to my lips and he licked his own, drawing the top one into his mouth and biting it. I think I fainted a little, which I know isn't possible—one does not *faint a little*. But his sexy lip-lick-suck-bite thing may have caused a head rush.

I thought he was going to kiss me, because he was staring at my mouth in such a way that lead me to believe he was hungry…for my lips. He appeared to be struggling, warring with himself; I held my breath.

The five seconds he hesitated proved to be the undoing of the potential kiss, because we were unceremoniously interrupted by a shrieking Sam.

"What the hell is going on?"

[6]
CHEMICAL KINETICS

"FOOLISH, ABSURD, BRAINLESS, crazy, preposterous, ridiculous, silly, stupid…," I muttered.

"What are you doing?"

I slid my eyes to my right where surly faced Sam sat, flipping through her political science textbook pretending to study.

"You know what I'm doing," I whispered.

"It's the synonym game, isn't it?" she whispered back, turning just slightly in her seat and dipping her head close to mine. "What's the word?"

"Foolish."

"Oh. How many do you have so far?"

"Uh, seven I think, maybe eight."

"Well…you need more than that." Sam turned and glanced over her shoulder.

I had the window seat. She had the aisle seat. Therefore, the boys were behind her. I'd achieved maximum willpower and hadn't looked at Martin for the last forty-five minutes. If this were a video game, I'd be on level one thousand, about to face the final boss, and my palms would be sweating with the anticipation.

My palms were sweating now.

Not looking at Martin every thirteen seconds was torture. He was so…lookable. And *lookable* wasn't even a word. It should have been, because he was definitely it. Easy-on-the-eyes was the closest phrase I could come up with that would be synonymous with the non-word *lookable*. Maybe mesmerizing?

Mesmerizing, hypnotic, irresistible, alluring, seductive… Hmm…

"Did you know that deductive and seductive are only one letter away from being the same word?" I asked.

Sam turned back to me and gave me a slight stink eye. "And conducive is conductive, but without a T."

"Huh." I nodded. That was interesting. I wondered how many –ductive words I could identify.

Sam continued on a whisper, "Are you ready to talk about it yet?"

"Talk about what?" I removed my eyes from her and stared at the vacant seat in front of mine. Since we were on Martin's dad's private plane, we had tons of space. Two seats were on each side of the aisle, and the plane had six rows with an open seating area in the back that included a bar, couches, and a big screen TV. In the front cabin, every other row faced backward which resulted in four seats facing each other.

When we boarded the plane, Sam insisted she and I needed all four of our seats and that neither Martin nor any of his boy-entourage were allowed to sit across from us. Since finding Martin hovering over me earlier in our dorm room, with clear intent-to-kiss posturing, Sam had been doing a lot of insisting.

Sam leveled me with a narrowed glare. "Don't play dumb, Kaitlyn Parker. Why are we on this plane?"

I folded my arms on my knees and buried my head in my arms.

I felt her tugging on my hair, not hard, just trying to get me to sit up. I didn't. A moment later she was leaning over me, whispering in my ear, "When I walked in on you this morning you were about to do something *imprudent*. Is that one on your list of synonyms for foolish?"

"No. I'll add it to the list." My response was muffled because I was hiding.

"Parker, why are we on this plane?"

I stared at the fabric of the jeans covering my legs within the dim cavern created by my head, arms, and hair. Blowing out a long, measured breath, I sat up slowly, straightening until my back was resting against the seat cushion again and my eyes were level with surly faced Sam.

I stared at her. She stared back, expectant.

"I promised him," I said.

Her eyebrows bounced up then down. "You promised him? That's it, that's why we're here? You promised?"

I nodded. "Yes. I promised him. I promised him last night and I promised him this morning and then you walked in and you freaked out and then he freaked out and then I thought about hiding in the closet, but I don't own any spiky heels, so I just agreed. Okay? I just agreed so the freak outs and the name calling would cease and desist."

Sam's eyes were half-lidded and her continued surly expression told me she was not impressed with my answer.

But it was the truth…kind of.

When Sam walked in, she'd pitched a fit and started yelling at Martin. Really, she overreacted because she loves me. She was pretty nasty to Martin, called him some unpleasant names I won't repeat, but I will say they are synonyms for whoreson.

Then Martin, who has no problem yelling at females, males, turtles, grass, and furniture, yelled back. Really, he was defending himself from her overprotectiveness and nasty name-calling. To his credit, he didn't call her any names. Mostly he just told her to back off and to *"mind her own goddamn business."*

I stepped in and tried to calm them both down. In doing so, I reassured Martin that I would be going with him—because I did promise him more than once—but only if Sam could go too. Eventually he overcame the shock of my request and agreed. Once he confirmed our destination would have a tennis court, Sam agreed.

Then he did something weird.

He gathered me up in his arms like I belonged there, gave me a swift, closed-mouth kiss, and said he'd wait for me in the hall. Then he left the room and stepped out of the suite area and promptly waited…in the hall…for me…for a full hour.

I felt like Scarlett O'Hara after she was kissed by Rhett Butler, confused and anxious and swoony and wanting it to happen again.

Sam and I had a brief argument after that, and by some miracle she agreed to come with me. Honestly, I don't think she felt like she had a choice since I stubbornly insisted I was going, and she lacked the time necessary to argue me out of it.

However, all the arguing and promising and name-calling aside, a large part of me was strangely excited about the trip. I was nineteen years old and the dodgiest thing I'd ever done was drink peach schnapps and drunk dial my ex last summer. I'd never thrown caution to the wind before. I'd never done anything this nutty and spontaneous. It was equal parts thrilling, terrifying, and confusing.

So…here we were. On the plane, with Martin, his handsome friend Eric from the fraternity party, and seven other dudes, most of whom looked like they'd stepped out of an Abercrombie and Fitch photo-shoot; except they had clothes on, unfortunately. Sam and I were the only females if you didn't count the two flight attendants.

We'd been briefly introduced to the boys upon entering the plane. Martin had referred to a few of them by a number first, then by first name.

Interestingly, they didn't seem to be surprised by our presence. I was also pretty sure they were checking me out, but not in the, *I might hit that* checking me out. More like a, *Are you a Yoko Ono?* checking me out.

As I shook everyone's hand I was surprised to see that one of the seven guys was Ben, the cuss monster from my time spent in the science cabinet. I couldn't fathom why Martin would have him come along, especially given the fact he'd tried to drug then extort Martin the night before.

Maybe they'd man-hugged it out.

Boys were just weird.

I made a mental note to tell Martin the entire conversation between Ben and the unknown female, because Ben had basically admitted to drugging girls. And there was really only one reason he could be drugging girls. He was Ben the rapist as far as I was concerned and I wanted nothing to do with him.

Sam and I took a seat in the front of the plane after introductions and left the males to their bonding.

I felt the mounting pressure of Sam's glare; she pressed her lips together in my general direction, looking displeased and surly.

"I can't believe we did this, I can't believe I let you talk me into this. How did that happen? How did we get here? And now we're going to some private beach in the middle of the Caribbean? This is crazy."

"It is kind of crazy." I shrugged, feeling shell shocked by the fact I was on this plane and all the circumstances leading up to this moment. Less than twenty-four hours ago I'd kissed Martin Sandeke—or rather, he'd kissed me. And then it happened again…and again. He'd placed his hands on my body like he had a right to do so, and I let him.

My skin still remembered his touch. Just thinking about his hands on me made my breasts feel tight and heavy, and my neck, back, and arms break out in goosebumps. I was warm all over and felt a little drunk with excitement and fear.

"But," I started, stopped, gave my head a quick shake, then began again, "but…it's okay. We're okay. We're together. If we get there and we don't want to stay we can leave."

"And go where? Do what? Swim to Jamaica?"

I shook my head, fighting back the swelling tide of Martin-inspired lust.

"No. I sent George, my mother's PA, a message. George knows the flight information, where we are. Worst case scenario, I call him and he arranges for us to leave. We're good."

Sam looked at me for several soundless seconds, then blurted, "You told your mother?"

"Of course. Well, technically I told her personal assistant, George. As the daughter of a senator I have to inform her any time I leave the country."

"You don't think she's going to freak out?"

63

"No. Why would she? I'm using the buddy system. She knows where I am, and with whom, and for how long, and why."

Although, I was still a bit uncertain as to why...

"You ladies need any drinks?"

Both Sam and I glanced up to find handsome Eric hovering in the aisle, poised at the precipice to our secluded island of four seats. Sam stared at him, like she was confused by his presence.

"What?" she asked.

"Drinks. Do you need any…drinks?"

"No. No drinks." She crossed her arms and tilted her head to the side, her eyes narrowing as though she were inspecting him. "You're shorter than I remembered."

He returned her eye squint and raised her a smirk. "Maybe you're suffering from altitude sickness. You should probably get up and walk around, stretch your legs."

More squint staring ensued and now they were both smirking.

At length, Sam nodded and said, "I could stretch my legs."

I eyeballed her as she quickly unbuckled her seatbelt and stood, all the while her gaze affixed to handsome Eric. His smirk became a grin when she stepped into the aisle and his eyes visibly brightened when she moved a tad closer to him.

"Let me give you a tour of the plane," he offered helpfully like a boy scout. "You can lean on me if we experience any turbulence."

"Sure thing," she drawled, sounding surly and amused at the same time. "Lead the way, shorty."

Eric rubbed the back of his neck and breathed a laugh as the two of them walked off together to the front of the plane. I craned my neck and watched them depart with borderline rapt fascination.

When Sam laughed at something Eric said I could watch no longer without labeling myself a creeper. So I relaxed—as much as I could relax—back in my seat and stared at my hands.

"Parker."

I jumped at the sound of my name coming from Martin's lips and turned to face him. I also, for reasons known only to my subconscious, balled my hands into fists and lifted them between us, like I was prepared for a fist fight or a boxing match.

He studied my defensive posturing and smirked, taking the seat Sam had vacated without asking permission. Meanwhile I glared at him, my mental wall up and prepped, though my hands fell back to my lap. I had to do this because…super-hot boy alert level ten thousand.

"Sandeke," I said. I knew I sounded ridiculous, like I was greeting a sworn enemy, but I had to be on guard.

His gaze skated over my face then flickered to my hands, still fists on my lap. Then he gave my hands a smile. Apparently they amused him.

"Are you going to hit me?"

"I don't know," I answered honestly. "It depends on if you take your pants off again."

"You'll hit me if I take my pants off?"

"Yeah…I might give you a junk punch."

He laughed, very loudly and very suddenly, and with the complete abandon that comes from being surprised. But his laugh was a radioactive seduction and had a half-life of infinity. I wanted him to stop laughing never. It made his eyes crinkle and his mouth curve in a sinful smile, showcasing his excellent dental hygiene regimen.

He also looked so different. He usually wore an expression of perpetual unimpressed boredom. Perpetual unimpressed boredom was a good look for him, a very good look. As were all the other expressions I'd seen, like distrust, mischievous amusement, thunderous anger, unveiled interest, etc.

But laughter…he almost looked happy. Happiness on Martin was a revelation of beauty and physical perfection married to excellent and infectious good-mood vibes. I let my fists drop. Less than a minute into our first interaction on this trip and my carefully constructed defenses had been virtually blown to bits.

I might as well wave the white panties of surrender.

"Oh, well. Barnacles," I said to nothing and no one.

His laugh gradually receded and his eyes flickered over me. "No more fists."

"Nope. There's no use." I'm sure I sounded despondent.

"So you think I could take you in a fist fight?"

"I think you could take me whenever." I shrugged. "If you wanted to, and I really only have myself to blame."

Martin narrowed his eyes, and they sharpened, surveying me. "You don't look happy about this."

"I'm not."

"Why not?"

I stared at him for a beat then freely admitted the truth. "Here is the problem, Martin. I feel like I like you."

The sharpness in his gaze softened and his mouth curved into a lazy, satisfied smile. "That doesn't sound like a problem to me."

"But it is," I pressed. "Because the feeling originates entirely in my pants."

Martin choked a shocked laugh, and leaned away from me.

I rushed to continue. "Hence the problem, you see? I know you as my lab partner who won't help me tabulate findings. And I also know you as a bit of a—and pardon the expression—as a bit of a manwhore who is not nice to the girls he sleeps with and who gets into fist fights, and who is somewhat bitter and jaded despite having the world at his fingertips."

Martin clenched his jaw. His eyelids drooped into unhappy slits and he flinched just slightly. His long fingers tightened on his legs.

I ignored the outward signs of irritation, wanting to make him see reason. "We have nothing in common. You're in a fraternity, go to parties *on purpose*, own a yacht, and are the king of the universe." I pressed both of my hands to my chest. "And I'm an unapologetic nerd who thinks it's fun to spend Saturday nights playing my guitar and writing music. I like arguing about Doctor Who episodes, and whether Samwise Gamgee or Frodo Baggins was ultimately responsible for the destruction of the ring. I play video games. I limit myself to three cookies, but then always cheat and have seven. Meanwhile you look like you've never had a cookie in your life. I'm a virgin and you're only the second boy I've kissed… We just don't fit." I said this last part quietly, gently, hoping he'd see reason.

Martin's face was devoid of expression, but his gaze moved from the tip of my chin to the top of my forehead, then back to my eyes.

He was smiling…sorta. But it resembled a grimace more than a smile. I watched his chest expand with a deep breath before he said, "You don't even know me, how can you say we don't fit? That's not right, Kaitlyn."

"I—"

"The way you describe me makes me sound like an entitled asshole."

It was my turn to flinch, lean away. My cheeks heated and stung as though they'd been slapped. I gaped at him and his fierce blue eyes for a long stretch. When he said nothing more, just glared at me, I ducked my head and studied the armrest between us.

"I. I. I…you're right," I admitted on a sigh. "I don't know you, not really. And you're right that my conclusion we don't fit is based on my observations and assumptions, which are clearly limited to empirical data sources."

"I'm not suggesting marriage, Parker. I just…" He paused, though I felt his gaze on me and it felt heavy. "Look at me."

I braced myself, then lifted my chin to meet his eyes. I expected to find a glower or a scowl. Instead I found his stare to be oddly earnest and searching.

"I'd just like a chance to know you."

"But why?" I blurted, feeling offended on behalf of everything that was perfect and gifted and beautiful about him. "Why me?"

"Because you're not intimidated by me."

"Well, that's wrong. I am. You scare me."

"No, I don't."

"You kind of do."

"No, I don't. That feeling of fear and excitement? *That* originates in your pants. It isn't about who I am, it's about what I look like. I feel that for you too."

My brain stumbled to grasp his meaning. I lifted an eyebrow, pursed my lips, and considered this statement.

He continued before I was finished considering. "You don't care about my family."

"I care about your family as human beings, but I don't know your family," I said defensively. "I'm sure if I knew them I'd care about them."

"Exactly. That's exactly right, except you wouldn't. If you knew my family you wouldn't care about them, because you're smart." The cloudy frustration in his eyes began to dissipate and he looked like my answer pleased him.

"That's true. I am smart. But you are also smart, maybe smarter."

"And you're funny."

"You should know that most of the time the funny is not on purpose."

"And honest."

"That's not always a good thing."

"And fucking gorgeous—"

I paired a huff with dismissive snort-laugh. But then my expression sobered when I saw Martin was serious.

I swallowed with difficulty then cleared my throat. I couldn't quite bear the weight and intensity of his stare, so I glanced down again at the arm rest. I'd learned from my mother that when someone gives you a subjective compliment—meaning one that can't be disproven and is based on opinion—but that you find to be completely false, rather than argue, it's much better to just say *thank you,* or *I appreciate that* and strive to be that compliment.

Fools fight compliments, she'd said, and sometimes other people see you better than you can see yourself.

So I quietly said, "Thank you," to the armrest.

"You're welcome."

I tucked my hair behind my ears and wrestled to find the courage to look at him again. I made it as far as his neck.

"Are you going to give me a chance? Yes or no?" The way he spoke, with such severe directness, was off-putting and strangely alluring. He was entitled, or at least he came across that way, because all of his words were demands.

It also made me want to refuse what he was demanding.

"I'm…going to be open to the possibility of giving you a chance." When I finished, my eyes flickered to his. I discovered him watching me with a narrowed stare and a little smirk. He was really too freaking good-looking, it was the un-fairest of the unfair.

"Is that the best you can do?" he challenged, leaning forward.

"No. But how you speak to me sometimes makes me want to withhold what you want."

His eyes flashed and felt at once more penetrating. "How do I speak to you?"

"Like I owe you something, like you're entitled."

"That's just confidence. I'm not going to be self-conscious for any reason, and I'm not going to fake it to make you feel better."

His response was jarring, irritating, and oddly thrilling, so I volleyed back, "Maybe you should be. Maybe your confidence isn't based on reality. Maybe you're not infallible. Maybe you're not always going to get what you want."

He watched me as several long moments passed, his gaze growing increasingly inscrutable but somehow hotter. I held his eyes, maybe finding the courage because my feathers were ruffled.

"Okay," he finally said. "I'll try not to demand things of you…as often."

"Good." I felt strangely disappointed at this news, which made no sense. Did I enjoy it when he spoke to me like I was an underling assigned to obey his every whim? When I reflected on it I realized that maybe I did, because I certainly enjoyed rebelling, defying, and challenging his demands...

We stared at each other. I tried to look at him and his beautiful face with as much objectivity as possible. Who was this person? Who was Martin Sandeke really?

"Tell me something, Martin."

"What do you want to know, Parker?" Again my question seemed to please him, his features softening and settling into amused—dare I say enthusiastic?—curiosity.

"What do you think about the Samwise Gamgee versus Frodo Baggins debate?"

His smile flattened just a little and for the first time since he sat down, Martin glanced away. He cleared his throat, picked at a spot on his jeans, then returned his gaze to mine. "I have no idea what you're talking about."

This admission made me smile, then laugh belatedly because he looked uncomfortable. Martin Sandeke looked uncomfortable and it was because he was out of his depth, specifically, he was out of his nerd depth, and being out of his depth looked adorable on Martin.

"Well, let me enlighten you," I said with a bit of show-womanship, waving my hand through the air. I then turned toward him completely. I didn't try to dim my bright smile. "There is this book, it is called Lord of the Rings and it was written by a linguist w-a-a-a-a-y back in the twentieth century."

"I've heard of the Lord of the Rings." His lips twitched but his tone was deadpan. I took this as a good sign.

"Ah, good. Have you seen the movies?"

"No."

"But you've heard of the twentieth century? It came right after the nineteenth century."

He didn't respond, but his closed-mouth smile grew. His fathomless blue eyes were at half-mast, aquamarine, and glittering like the ocean at sunset.

"I'll take that as a yes. Anyway, in this book there are different kinds of races—elves, orcs, humans, blah, blah, blah, dwarves—but also, there is this race of beings called hobbits. They are little, short of stature, and usually considered insignificant. They have furry feet and they like to smoke pipes and live quietly. In fact, they live very quietly. But they have several breakfasts daily, so…awesome. Anyway…"

Martin cocked his head to the side as though studying me. I didn't know if he were actually listening or not, but his eyes were intent and focused, like I was providing him with a super important riddle he would have to solve at some point. It gave me fluttery butterflies in my stomach to have his complete attention like this. It also reminded me how much that area in my pants liked him.

"Anyway," I repeated, trying to focus. "The whole point of the book is to destroy this ring, because the ring is very, very bad."

"Why is it bad?"

"You'll have to read the book, and don't interrupt me. It's distracting enough looking at you. You've already derailed my brain train with your face several times."

Martin's mouth pressed together more firmly and I got the impression he was trying not to laugh.

"Back to the story, ultimately—spoiler alert—the ring is destroyed by two of these hobbits."

Both of his eyebrows jumped in surprise. "How did they do that? You said they're insignificant."

"Like I said, you'll have to read the book for the specifics, but the crux of my question has to do with the two hobbits who destroy the ring—Frodo and Samwise. Frodo bears the ring. He carries it. But," I lifted a finger in the air for emphasis, "Samwise is his trusted servant, and he is very trustworthy. He supports Frodo, he keeps Frodo from giving up. He even bears the ring for a short time. Plus there's this bit at the very end that…well, you'll have to read the book. So, the question is—who deserves the credit for the destruction of the ring? Who was stronger? Frodo or Samwise? The master or the servant?"

Martin frowned at me; I took it as a good sign because it meant he was actually considering the question. But then his frown started to worry me because his eyes grew cagey and guarded.

After a few minutes he asked, "Is this a test?"

I lifted an eyebrow at him and his tone. He sounded a little angry.

"What do you mean?"

"Just what I said, is this a test? If I answer incorrectly are you still going to give us a chance?"

Yep. Definitely angry.

It was my turn to frown. "Martin, it's a conversation. We're just having a conversation. This isn't a test. You said, and I agree, that I don't know you very well. This is my attempt to get to know you better."

"But if I answer in a way you don't like, what happens?"

I stared at him, my features likely showing my disorientation at his odd question. "Um," my eyes flickered to the side, because I was trying not to look at him like he was a crackhead, "nothing? I mean, we talk about it, each reviewing our own opinions and providing support for what we believe. But then, we can always agree to disagree at some point."

"Then after that?"

"I guess we could end it with a high five to show that there are no hard feelings...?"

His eyes narrowed at me, and he was looking at me like I was the puzzle; when he spoke next it was with an air of distraction. "That sounds nice."

I frowned, considering him, considering his reaction to a simple question. It made me wonder whether or not Martin Sandeke had ever had a conversation before, one where he was allowed to disagree without being made fun of or punished for his thoughts, where it wasn't a test.

I was about to ask him something along these lines when the pilot's voice came over the intercom. He announced we were approaching the airport, and should buckle in for our final descent. Meanwhile, I blinked at Martin and a dawning and disturbing realization took root.

Martin Sandeke wasn't used to freely voicing his thoughts and feelings...nor was he used to kindness.

[7]

MOLECULAR GEOMETRY AND BONDING THEORIES

MUCH OF SAM'S surly mood dissipated after her fifteen-minute plane tour courtesy of the handsome Eric. I was both pleased and distressed by this turn of events. Since Sam's attention was redirected—or best case scenario, it was split between me and Eric—this meant she wasn't quite as focused on her role as my spring break chastity belt.

A very luxurious stretch limo picked us up. Inside the car, I sat next to one of the seven other guys; his name was Ray, and his parents had immigrated from Mumbai, India, when he was two. He was a biochemistry major, and he was five seat.

"Five seat?" I asked, my head titling to the side. "What do you mean five seat?"

Two more of the boys entered the limo, sitting on the bench across from Sam and Eric.

"Five seat in the crew boat. I'm a starboard," Ray explained, flashing me a big smile when he saw I didn't quite understand what he meant. "We're all on the crew team together, in the same boat. I'm five seat, Martin is eight seat. He's the stroke at the stern, the back of the boat." Ray lifted his chin toward one of the other guys. "That's our coxswain, Lee."

I gave Lee a friendly smile. "What's a cocks-twin?"

Lee chuckled and shook his head. "It's pronounced cox-wain, not cocks-twin. Basically, I steer the boat and keep these guys from being lazy assholes."

"Lee also gets to stare into Stroke's dreamy blue eyes all day," Ray added with a grin. "You should probably be jealous."

I shrugged my shoulders convulsively, feeling acutely weird and self-conscious. "What...I...we...it's...I mean...what are you talking about?" I sputtered as my hands did weird things, jerky movements in the air in front of me. "I'm not jealous. Why would I be jealous? I don't even know the guy."

Ray, Lee, Eric, and another of the guys whose name was Herc—who had obscenely large leg muscles—all lifted their eyebrows at me in unison.

"You're his girl, right?" Lee glanced at his teammates as though to confirm his statement.

"That's right," Herc confirmed, his tone sure and steady.

I felt Sam tug at my shirt but I ignored her. At that moment three of the other guys entered the car; I'd recognized two of them as the pair of brown-eyed frat boys who'd been with Eric at the party the night before. The taller of the two, Griffin, had been handsy with me at the frat house. The other one, Will, had hit Griffin on the back of the head as they'd walked away.

The other guy's name was Tambor. He had blond hair, darker than Ben's, longish with pale highlights likely caused by the sun. He had deep brown eyes and an exceedingly stoic face. He and Herc were the shortest and the stockiest of the boys at an approximate and *measly* six foot one.

"So...where does everyone else sit? In the boat, I mean," I asked weakly, wanting to change the subject.

"As you know, Martin is stroke, which is eight seat." Ray then pointed to Eric. "Eric is a starboard, seven seat. Ben," he paused and looked around the inside of the vehicle. Ben and Martin were the only two not in the car yet. "Well, Ben who isn't here is port, seat six. We've already established that I'm starboard five seat. Griffin is behind me, port four seat. Then Will, starboard three seat. Tambor, port second seat. Last but not least is Herc. He's the bow, first seat, in the front of the boat."

"All the even seats are port seats, and the odds are starboard?"

Ray nodded. "That's right. Port and starboard have to do with the sides of the boat. My oar is rigged on the starboard side; whereas Martin's, Ben's, Griffin's, and Tambor's are rigged on the port side."

I nodded, picturing a crew boat I'd seen on TV during the summer Olympics. Now, considering how Martin had originally introduced everyone on the plane—referring to each of them as a number first before their names—this made a lot more sense. Their nicknames were their seat assignments, with Martin called Stroke and Herc called Bow.

Martin entered the limo just as Ray finished explaining port and starboard. I noted that a hush fell over the occupants; everyone seemed to sit a little straighter, the guys looking to him as though called to attention.

His did a sweep of the interior as Ben entered through the other door and shut it. Martin's gaze paused on me, which sent heat to my cheeks and set off a buzzing in my stomach. Eventually he glared at Ray and his eyes narrowed by an infinitesimal margin.

Ray's answering smile looked cautious. "I'll just move over this way..." Ray scooched away from me, leaving plenty of room for someone to fill the void.

Martin followed Ray's movements with his eyes, stared at him for a beat, then ducked and crossed to the now vacant seat next to mine. Martin then cast a dark glare around the limo, almost like he was warning them off his Chinese takeout leftovers.

Meanwhile I pressed my lips into an unhappy line. I was unimpressed with the dynamic of unspoken, but clearly understood, possessiveness.

Even if I were Martin's girl—which I wasn't—there was nothing amiss with me sitting next to Martin's friend. I felt abruptly as though I'd just been peed on.

I didn't want to be peed on.

* * *

THE REST OF the journey was eventfully uneventful. The limo's journey to the marina was fifteen minutes. At the marina, men appeared—as though from nowhere—and loaded our belongings onto a boat. Then the men disappeared. The boat journeyed forty-five minutes to another, much smaller marina situated on a spec of an island.

At least it looked like a spec at first. Upon closer inspection, I estimated it was about four miles long and at least a mile wide. The lush tropical forests were dotted with obscenely massive luxury homes—some directly on the beach, some higher up on hilly cliffs. I counted seven as we circled to the dock.

We then loaded into five all-terrain golf cart-like vehicles, two per vehicle. I traveled with Martin, Sam traveled with Eric. We traversed a well-maintained dirt road to where I surmised we'd be staying for the next week.

I didn't bring up Martin's inappropriate behavior; this was for several reasons. First, drama repelled me. I didn't want to start a conversation on the topic when others could overhear. Therefore I just put up with his hovering and the way he would stare down the other guys when they'd enter my radius.

Second, I didn't know how to start the dialogue. What if I was imagining things? What if I was being overly sensitive? What if this was what normal relationships were like? If we'd actually been dating, I think I might have been able to navigate through the conversation, but we weren't.

"Why are you so quiet?"

I'd been wrapped up in my thoughts and started a little at his bluntly spoken question.

"Uh." I glanced at him. He was splitting his attention between me and the road. "Because I'm thinking about something."

"What are you thinking about?" he asked. As usual it sounded like a demand.

I tried not to read too much into the tone of his voice; maybe

Martin didn't know how to ask nicely, another thing I didn't like very much about him.

"I guess because I don't have much experience with boys, so I'm trying to figure something out."

"What is it? Maybe I can help." He nudged me with his elbow.

I shook my head, not ready to talk about it yet. "I'm not ready to discuss it. I need some time with my thoughts."

His intelligent eyes flicked over me, his expression growing distant and impassive. At length he shrugged, grim-faced, and gave his attention wholly to the road. We didn't speak again until we arrived at the house.

And by house I mean not a house at all. It was a behemoth.

Once inside I marveled at the opulence. The giant foyer steps were a blue marble, resembling turquoise, with inlay brass. A grandiose and gracefully curving staircase dominated the left side of the entrance, while a three-story single-paned window provided natural light and a breathtaking view of the ocean beyond. In the center of the space was a wide fountain with a surprisingly tasteful sculpture of a mermaid blowing water out of a conch shell.

Everything was overly detailed. The wooden carvings on the staircase had carvings. The brass inlay danced beautiful oceanic patterns over the floor. Glorious mosaics of blue and copper decorated the fountain.

It was all too much. It didn't feel like a house, it felt like the lobby for a huge, swanky hotel.

When I realized I was gaping, I snapped my mouth shut and glanced at Martin to see if he'd caught my oddball display of horrified amazement. He had. He was glaring at me. Again.

I was starting to wonder if I'd imagined his laugh back on the plane and if he were capable of anything other than heavily-lidded severe stares. Don't get me wrong, he still looked heavenly even when he was administering heavily-lidded severe stares, but that was only if one wasn't the recipient of said stare.

I was on the receiving end now, his focus on me, and he looked unhappy.

Therefore I gave him a buggy-eyed nose scrunch, followed by a full-on weird face—tongue out, eyes crossed, teeth bared like a rabbit —and then refocused on his features to see if it had made any effect.

It had. Now he was looking at *me* like I was a crackhead.

"Parker, what are you doing?"

"Making a funny face in an effort to make you stop staring at me like I murdered your beloved goldfish. What are *you* doing?"

I was pleased to see his eyes lighten with something like confused wonder, but before he could speak, the sound of voices entering the house pulled my attention back to the massive doors. I opened my mouth to announce where we were, but the words never came because Martin put his hand over my mouth—abruptly but gently—bringing my attention back to him.

He put a finger to his lips in the universal symbol for *shhh* then fit his hand in mine and pulled me around the fountain, down a hall, beyond the massive, three-story window overlooking the sea, through a large living room with a giant fireplace—fireplace? On a tropical Island? Rich people were crazy—and into a massive bedroom suite done all in sterile whites and shades of blue and sea-green.

He shut the solid teak door then backed me up against it, staring down at me, holding me in place with his eyes and the promise they held. My heart thudded painfully in my chest and I was drowning in his intense focus.

I opened my mouth again to say something, anything really, but it was lost because he was kissing me. The hot, urgent slickness of his tongue robbing me of my breath, his solid body against mine warming me beyond the humid stickiness of the tropics, permeating to my center.

We kissed and kissed then kissed some more. It wasn't until he tore his mouth from mine that I realized I was holding fistfuls of his hair and was on my tiptoes.

His forehead met mine and he growled, a low sound laced with frustration, before he said, "You are too fucking cute."

"You too."

He exhaled a disbelieving breath, and swallowed. "I'm cute?"

"As a button."

He chuckled, stealing another kiss. "I wish we were here alone. I wish…God, I just want you to myself."

A prickle of unease made the short hairs of my neck stand at attention. On one hand, it was a lovely thing for him to say. On the other hand, he'd just figuratively urinated a circle around me in his blatant display of caveman possessiveness. Maybe I was overreacting, but I had no baseline for comparison. This was all very, very new territory for me.

I needed time to think, away from his lips *and* mesmerizing looks.

Luckily, I was pretty certain this place had some nice closets.

* * *

"HE'S THE ALPHA MALE." Sam said this from my bed where she lay with her arms and legs spread out. I was next to her, my arms and legs also spread.

We weren't touching. The bed should have had its own zip code.

After my lovely kisses with Martin, he informed me that the gargantuan and beautiful suite was mine. The voices of our co-travelers grew louder, closer, and so he told me to stay put. He explained people would be bringing in my luggage as well as food. Then he left.

People did arrive with my bags. Again, random people seemed to appear out of thin air—an older man in a suit directed a younger man where to place my things. Then a woman about ten years older than me showed up with a tray of decadent food, sparkling mineral water, and asked if she could draw me a bath or arrange for a massage.

I politely refused both, but insisted on introducing myself to these apparitions. Ultimately I had to press them for names because at first they offered me only titles.

The older man was the staff director - Mr. Thompson.

The younger man was one of the groundskeepers - Peter.

The woman was the house manager - Mrs. Greenstone.

I tried to modulate my tone to offhanded and nonchalant as I asked how many other staff members were present at the house. After Mr.

Thompson listed the cook, cook's aide, three other groundskeepers, and two maids, I stopped counting. The house staff outnumbered the guests.

Sam found me just as Mr. Thompson was taking his leave.

That's right, taking his leave...like some grand butler from regency England. I'd entered the bizzaro world of the obscenely rich where baths were drawn and leave was taken.

Now Sam and I were munching on the tray of food and staring at the vaulted ceiling. An immense, beautiful skylight showed me the late afternoon sky was a cloudless blue.

Sam continued voicing her theory while munching on grapes. "You know, like a pack of wolves. He's their alpha."

I grimaced and twisted my lips to the side to hide my expression, not that she was looking at me.

"That's silly," I said.

"No, it's totally not. They all...well...they all basically worship him, I think. Eric said that eight seat, Martin's position, is arguably the most important seat in the boat. He sets the rhythm for the rest of the boat, pushes them. Even Lee, who *freaking* steers the boat, follows his lead. They do what are called 'power tens' during practices and races. It's where they all row as hard as they can for ten strokes—well, Martin decides when and for how long. He's only a sophomore and he has the most coveted spot on the team, *and* he's team captain. The rest of the guys are juniors and seniors."

"Maybe it's because he's from such a fancy family," I said flippantly, because Sam was starting to make it sound like this stuff mattered. Granted, she was a competitive athlete, therefore I could forgive some of her wide-eyed expression and excitement in her voice.

Whereas I'd never understood sports and team dynamics. I'd tried playing soccer once; everyone was so serious about it. I kept thinking how silly it was to run around a grassy field, kick a ball into a net, and think of it as an accomplishment.

Finishing War and Peace, now that was an accomplishment.

"No, I asked Eric how Martin got his seat," Sam said, turning to face me, her elbow and hand propping up her head. "He said Martin has the best erg time—it has to do with the rowing machine they use, the ergometer or whatever it's called—and that he has the best form *by far*. Honestly, it's like Eric is brainwashed or has a crush on him or something. They talk about him like he invented the sport."

I shrugged, but my mind was caught on the "pack of wolves" metaphor, Martin as an alpha to a pack of hard-bodied rowers. It might explain why every time he spoke it sounded like a demand. As well, it explained the pack mentality in the limo and on the boat. He was younger than they were. I wondered if all his dazzling wealth had anything to do with why he was able to command their respect so completely.

I could feel Sam's eyes on me. I kept my attention focused on the sky.

After a while she said, "You are beautiful, you know."

My eyes jumped to hers and I automatically frowned, her earnestly spoken words catching me off guard.

"What you talkin' 'bout, Willis?"

She gave me a little smile then pushed on my shoulder. "You, being beautiful. You are beautiful. You don't focus on your looks or even seem to care about them, but you're really quite spectacular to look at."

I turned my head completely toward her and folded my hands on my stomach. "And you think this is why Martin is suddenly whisking me and my foul-mouthed friend off to private beaches? Because he thinks I'm beautiful?"

"It's definitely part of it. The boy has eyes and urges."

"Ha. Yes, he does..."

"But that's not why, or that's not all of it."

"Then what is it? Why am I here?"

Sam was quiet for a minute, then asked, "Why do you think?"

I glanced over her shoulder, my eyes resting on the magnificent view behind her. The entire back wall of the suite was glass and over-looked the beach. The house was some feet above sea level. If I'd been standing I would see the white, sandy shore. But from this vantage point, all I saw was blue sky kissing the blue ocean at the horizon.

"I think," I started, deciding to speak my thoughts out loud as they occurred to me. I needed to talk this through with someone and I needed to get out of my own head because I couldn't get any further than, *This makes no sense!*

"I think he wants someone to be nice to him," I blurted.

I brought Sam back into focus, saw her surprised expression, but then something like contemplation gripped her features.

I continued. "I think he's tired of people judging him or making assumptions about who he is based on who his family is. I think he wants someone to be nice to him, like him, and show interest in who he is because he's Martin, just Martin, and not because of who is family is, how much money he has...or what he looks like."

"That sounds...well, actually, that sounds plausible."

"I wonder," I propped myself up on my elbow, facing Sam and mirroring her position on the bed, "maybe he really just wants a friend. I think I could do that for him."

Her eyes narrowed on me. "I don't think he wants you to be his friend."

"But that's what he needs," I said, wrinkling my nose. "I think he trusts me because I don't want anything from him. I think he just really desperately needs someone to talk to, someone who is on his side, and he's confusing trust with...lust."

Sam smiled her amusement, her eyes dancing over my face. "Or he's confusing lust with trust."

I rolled my eyes and fell back to the bed, again staring out through the skylight.

"But seriously," she started, paused, then took a deep breath, "he's kind of possessive of you, right? Like, how he stared down Ray in the limo. And I thought he was going to bite Griffin's arm when he touched you while we were on the boat. It seems especially strange since you two aren't even really together yet."

Yet... O.o

"It is weird. I'm glad you said something because I wondered if I was just overreacting. And it's all so fast."

"No, not really. You've been lab partners for almost two semesters. From what you told me about your conversation with him against the pool table last night, for him, I think this relationship—in some form—has been going on for months, not hours. I suspect he's been thinking about you far more than you realize."

I covered my face with my hands. "How do I survive this? How am I going to get through this week? He needs a friend and all I can think about is doing very bad things to his body."

"You're starved for physical intimacy. He's starved for emotional intimacy. Maybe you can help him *and* help yourself."

"I don't want to use him like that. I think his whole life people have been trying to use him."

"I'm not talking about sex, Katy. I still don't think you're ready for that. You have a big heart and it would definitely get in the way of a no-strings arrangement. I'm just saying, there's nothing wrong with fooling around a little with a guy you're attracted to. Maybe…," Sam reached for my hands and pulled them away from my face. She then lifted her eyebrows and gave me a pointed look. "Maybe you can help each other."

[8]

BOND POLARITY AND ELECTRONEGATIVITY

S AM SPENT THE night with me. Having her there helped. But despite the heavenly bed and the sound of the ocean in the background, I didn't sleep very well.

Sam and I hadn't joined the boys for dinner. Instead we opted to sit on the balcony overlooking the sea and study. This was my idea. I needed more time to think, to consider, to plan my next move with Martin. I was certain he needed a friend much, much more than he needed a girlfriend, now I just needed to convince him of this fact.

Mr. Thompson stopped by to check in and make sure everything was to our liking. I asked about having dinner in the suite and he said he'd pass the message along. One of the maids brought us dinner. Her name was Rosa and she reminded me of my paternal grandmother; her big smile was sweet and she promised us cookies if we ate all our vegetables.

She also brought me a note from Martin. In his scrawling, masculine, chaotic script it read:

Parker,
I'll be down at the beach tonight. Come find me.
-Martin

I was relieved he didn't come by or press the issue of me taking dinner in my room. I needed space and time and…basically all the known dimensions available to me, maybe even the assistance of invisible dark matter. I wasn't ready for a moonlight stroll on the beach with Martin yet. The sky had too many stars to be anything but fatalistically romantic.

After eating, Sam and I studied some more. I opted for the giant shower with seven heads—despite the fact the bathtub was the size of a small swimming pool—then worked on a term paper until midnight when we went to bed.

It was early when I woke, the sun just making an appearance and the light still soft and hazy. I pulled on my bathrobe and walked to the window, wanting to catch the purples and oranges painting the sky before it surrendered to blue.

I got my wish and then some. The view was epically spectacular. The white sandy beach and calm water called to me in a way I'd never experienced. Suddenly, I wanted to go swimming. Right that minute. I needed to leave the manufactured luxury of the big house. The genuine beauty of nature called to me.

I quickly changed in the bathroom, careful to lather myself in super high SPF, and grabbed two oversized beach towels.

I also packed a canvas bag with a leftover bottle of water from the night before, my current book, a big hat, sunglasses, and other beach essentials. I exited out the balcony door and picked my way down the path to the beach. The path consisted of ten stone steps and a hundred feet of the finest, softest sand I'd ever touched.

Once there I dropped my belongings, discarded my T-shirt, cotton shorts, and flip flops, and walked into the salt water. The water was crystal clear, the temperature cool and refreshing, and was nearly as calm as a lake. It felt like heaven.

For at least an hour I floated, swam, searched for shells, and just generally enjoyed the alone time with my thoughts in this beautiful place. When my fingers became prunes, I reluctantly abandoned the water for the shore.

I arranged one of the towels under the shade of a big palm tree and rolled the other towel into a pillow for my head. Then, I read my book, drying in the sea air, and lazing about like a lazy person. This was the kind of unscheduled relaxing I'd embraced since starting college.

I was maybe four pages into my novel when I heard the noise; it was a chant—faint then louder—of baritone voices. Lifting onto my elbows, I set my book to one side, holding my place with my thumb, and peered around for the origin.

Then I saw them. All nine of the boys—looking remarkably like men—out some distance from shore; far enough away I couldn't quite make out individual faces, but close enough I could plainly see they were all shirtless. And it ought to be noted that they should always be shirtless. In fact, they should be disallowed from wearing shirts…ever.

They were rowing, their boat flying over the water. I strained my ears and realized they were counting backward from ten.

I followed their progress, marveling at how they moved so quickly and with seemingly so little effort in perfect unison. I wondered what that must be like, being part of something so perfect, so harmonious. It was…well, it was beautiful.

The closest I'd ever come to something like that was playing my music, losing myself on the piano, or jamming with my Sunday night bandmates. But we weren't perfect. We were far from harmonious, however sometimes we'd have a good night where everything felt right and effortless, like we were flying on the music we'd created together.

Just as suddenly as the rowers appeared they were gone. The boat went around the edge of the cove and their chant grew fainter, farther away. I stared at the spot where they'd disappeared for a minute then reclined back on my towel, watching the horizon.

"Holy crap. That was something."

I turned my head slightly and found Sam standing on the beach, her hands on her hips, and her attention focused on the bend of the cove. She was wearing an itsy bitsy bikini that showed how hard she worked on her tennis game.

"Hey, you there. Good-looking female," I called to her. "Why are you up?"

"Because I bought this damn bikini last year and this is my first chance to wear it." She sauntered over to where I reclined and spread out her towel. Her spot was somewhat in the sun, but I doubted she minded the opportunity to tan. I didn't want to take the chance of blinding someone, so I liked my spot in the shade. With my paper-white complexion, the glare off my thighs would likely burn retinas.

She turned to me to say something else, but then the chanting became audible again. Sure enough, the boat came back into view. Eight muscled rowers sweeping the water with their oars, Lee at the stern facing Martin. Their arms and shoulders flexing, their stomachs and backs rippling. The movement of their bodies was as mesmerizing as it was arousing. This time they were close enough I could almost see their facial expressions, see the sweat rolling down their necks and chests.

From where I sat, they looked stern, focused, maybe a little bit in pain, but still beautiful. Heart-achingly beautiful. My mouth went completely dry.

Sam and I watched them for almost a full minute before they flew past and were once more out of sight.

Then, she fanned herself. "Yeah. I am totally going to have sex with Eric. That was hot."

I said nothing, because once again my dirty thoughts were at odds with what I knew was smart, with what I knew was right.

Martin needed a friend.

I would be that friend.

I would.

And my pants hated me for it.

* * *

THREE OF THE groundskeepers brought brunch down to the beach under the oversight of Mrs. Greenstone. And by brunch, I mean they transported what looked like the equivalent of a fancy outdoor restaurant down to the beach. A large buffet was spread out on a huge wooden serving table, and beautifully carved dining tables and chairs with deep cushions were set up on the edge of the water. A sideboard with china, crystal, linen napkins, towels, suntan lotion—and basically everything else one might want for the beach—was set out with practiced and aesthetically pleasing efficiency.

To top it all off, several large arrangements of tropical flowers were placed on the tables along with little packets of aloe set on ice to chill.

I glanced sideways at the opulence, feeling out of place with my modest, black two-piece that was three years old, my turquoise Walmart flip flops, and my gas station sunglasses.

To be honest, the excess repelled me in much the same way the size and luxuriousness of the house had repelled me when we first arrived. I wasn't against people being rich. Nor was I against people owning and enjoying nice things.

I guessed the problem was that everything was too big, too much, too shiny, too new, too sterile, too impersonal. I felt like all the real details that mattered—the smell of the ocean, the sensation of sand beneath feet, the soft sounds of the sea meeting the shore, the rustle of wind through the palms—were lost in the ostentatiousness of the house and its sprawling splendiferous shadow.

Where Sam and I had set our towels was a good two hundred feet from the fancy buffet and beneath the shade of a palm; however, the spot was clearly visible from the trail. We were both on our stomachs and reading when Herc, Ray, and Ben appeared from the house path.

Ray gave us a little wave and an amiable smile, Herc gave us a little wave that I imagined was friendly for him, and Ben gave us a leering look and no other acknowledgement. I silently wondered again why Martin had invited Ben as all evidence pointed to the fact he was an unsavory sort. The guys crossed to the impressive brunch spread.

No sooner had they made it to the tables did Eric and Griffin jog past. Eric skidded to a stop when he saw us and gave Sam a bright smile. Griffin lifted his chin and waved politely, then made a beeline for the food.

"I'll be right back." Eric held out his index finger to us in the universal symbol for *give me a minute*. "I'm starving."

"Take your time." Sam shrugged, and I saw she was doing her best to appear unaffected. "It's not like we're going anywhere."

"Yeah. Good." Eric's eyes moved over her body—not in a leering,

I'd-hit-that kind of way, but rather in a *damn-you-must-work-out-and-I'm-impressed* kind of way—his eyebrows doing an adorable double jump of appreciation as he scanned her. Then he shook his head as though clearing it and slowly turned away. In fact, his steps were almost halting as he walked to the buffet yet turned back and glanced at Sam twice.

Sam, however, was looking at her book. But I could tell she wasn't reading. When he was out of earshot, she asked in a near whisper, "Did he look back?"

"Yes. Twice."

"Excellent."

I smirked and looked up at the guys. Unable to help herself, Sam lifted her eyes as well.

They hadn't bothered yet with shirts and were still clothed in spandex shorts that ended just above the knee. Really, they should have been naked. Their outfits left nothing to the imagination.

I quickly refocused attention on my book, my cheeks red from sudden exposure to male fineness, but Sam gaped for a few minutes longer.

"Thank you, Katy. Thank you for being Martin Sandeke's lab partner. Thank you for having no idea how amazing you are. Thank you for driving him wild with your clueless indifference. Just…thank you for this moment."

I rolled my eyes behind my sunglasses and flipped onto my back.

"You're welcome. Never say I didn't get you anything, especially since there are four more shirtless rowers on their way."

"I will die happy here, today, in this spot," she sighed.

"In your puddle of lust."

"Leave my puddle of lust alone. Get your own puddle."

A few moments passed in relative silence, relative because the sound of the boys' conversation drifted to us, though none of the words were decipherable. I was actually able to concentrate on my book for about ten minutes before we were interrupted.

"Hey, so what do you think so far?"

I turned my head and found Eric kneeling in the sand next to Sam's towel, splitting his attention between both of us. I rolled to my side then sat up, pulling my knees to my chest. Sam, however, continued to lounge on the ground.

"It's really nice," I said with feeling, because it was nice and he was being nice, and it's nice to be nice.

Then, because I wanted to say something more than just nice, I added, "The beach is exquisite. I've never seen this kind of sand."

Eric gave me a friendly smile. "Yeah, this is our second year. Last year Martin brought us down for spring break and I've been looking forward to it since we left. I love this place."

"I can see why," Sam said, "it's gorgeous."

Eric's gaze rested on her for a beat before he agreed, "Yeah, gorgeous…"

My eyes flickered between the two of them, obviously sharing a moment, and I tried not to make any sudden movements. I adverted my gaze to the cover of the book I'd discarded and realized I had no recollection of what I'd been reading.

Eric was the first to speak, and he did so with a charming grin. "So, Sam. Would you mind helping me put suntan lotion on my back? I'd like to go for a swim but I'm sure the stuff I put on earlier is mostly gone by now."

"Sure," she responded immediately, then hopped to her knees, grabbed her lotion, circled behind him as they both stood, and applied a generous amount of liquid SPF and UV protection to his torso.

He was facing me, so Sam was behind him. Therefore I was treated to her facial expressions while she touched his body. At one point she mouthed the words *Oh my God*, her eyes growing large. I had to roll my lips between my teeth to keep from laughing.

After the longest lotion lathering in the history of forever, Sam moved to step away but he caught her hand.

"Want to go swimming?"

She nodded, a big smile on her face. All her earlier attempts to keep it cool must have melted away…for some inexplicable reason.

Without a backward glance or a wave or an, *I'll see you later* in my direction, the two of them took off for the ocean. I watched them go feeling a mixture of excitement on Sam's behalf, and worry, also on Sam's behalf. She obviously liked him a lot. And I supposed he was likeable enough. But neither of us knew him very well.

"Hey. Kaitlyn, right?" someone said from behind me.

I turned toward the voice at my back and found Ben—the cuss monster, would-be drugger, self-admitted rapist, and blatant leerer—hovering at the edge of my towel. My stomach tightened with trepidation.

"Yes. That is correct. I am Kaitlyn," I said, not meaning to sound as robotic as I did but unable to help it. This guy wanted to hurt and extort Martin, and that alone was enough to make me dislike him with the heat of magma.

"Hey, so," his eyes moved over me again, where I was curled into a ball on my towel, "I need help getting this stuff on my back." He held up the bottle of suntan lotion Sam had just discarded.

"Okay…?" I peered at him, not understanding why he was telling me this.

We stared at each other for a beat. He was quite good-looking, very well built, very tall, and he made me exceedingly uneasy.

At length he huffed. "So, I need you to put the lotion on my back."

My frown deepened and I shook my head. "Um, no thanks."

"No thanks?"

"That is correct. No thanks."

His eyes darted between mine and he appeared to be confused. "You're not going to do it?"

"Correct. I'm not going to do it."

Ben's confused expression morphed into a sneer. "What's the big deal?"

I tightened my arms around my legs. "It's not a big deal. I don't touch people I don't know, it's one of my life rules." The nice thing about having life rules is that you can make up new ones on the spot when it's convenient. Not touching people I don't know hadn't been a life rule before this minute, but it was definitely on the list now.

"We've met."

"Yes, but I don't know you and I don't want to touch you."

He stared at me for five seconds, but it felt like an hour, his pale eyes growing mean and angry. Abruptly, he blurted, "Why are you being such a bitch about this? I just need some fucking help here and you're acting like a fucking bitch."

I flinched at the words—even his expletives were redundant and unimaginative—and then pulled my gaze from his, opting to stare at the beach and wishing I'd forced myself on Sam and Eric. They were in the water, floating, talking, and probably not cussing at each other.

Even though you don't feel calm doesn't mean you can't be calm. My mother's words came back to me.

"Go away," I said. My heartbeat and the pumping of my blood roared between my ears. My body was beyond tense, like it was bracing for a physical blow, and I felt abruptly cold and removed from my surroundings, like I was in a tunnel.

"Fine, fatty. I don't want your fucking chubby-ass fingers on me anyway."

I closed my eyes, waiting for the sound of his departure and trying to calm my heart. But he didn't leave. I felt him hovering there, just beyond the little island of safety that was my towel. I was about to launch myself up and away to the water, when he spoke again.

"Yeah, glad you're having a good time. This place is pretty great."

I frowned my confusion—which had momentarily paralyzed me—but didn't open my eyes.

But then Ben said, "Oh, hey Stroke," just as I discerned a new set of footsteps approaching from behind me. Martin was walking over.

I exhaled a slow breath, my insides still feeling like icicles, and slowly opened my eyes. I kept my attention affixed to the shore as I didn't want to look at this Ben person again, probably never.

"Hey," Martin said from someplace nearby and over my shoulder. "What's going on?"

"Ah, not much. Just keeping Kaitlyn company." Ben's voice was remarkably different, friendly, affable. "But since you're here, I'll just go grab some food. Do you want anything? Can I get you something?" Ben was obviously directing this solicitous question to Martin.

I wondered briefly if Martin should invest in a poison tester of some sort. I wouldn't trust Ben with a snake I didn't like, let alone to bring me food that wasn't tainted with arsenic.

"No," Martin said.

I nearly laughed, despite my brittle state. Martin's simple *no* sounded like so much more than a *no*. It sounded like a warning and a threat, like a dismissal and a command. I was impressed how much disdain he'd managed to pack into a single syllable word.

"Okay, well…" At last I heard Ben's feet move against the sand. "I'm starving so I'm going to eat. See you two later."

I remained still even when I was sure Ben had left. I couldn't quite pry my fingers from where they held my legs tightly tucked against me.

Growing up, I'd struggled a bit with my size, but not in the way most people approach size frustrations. I struggled and worked to accept it. I wished I could be different, yet because I trusted my mother and her assurances there was nothing wrong with me or the way I looked, that the baby fat was normal for me and that my body would shed it eventually, I never fought against the rolls.

I was a pudgy kid and very, very short through most of my childhood; then, during my sophomore year of high school, I stretched out and grew four inches basically overnight. I grew another two inches in my junior year.

But I've never been lean and firm; rather, I've always been soft and curved. I did rather like the line of my waist, however, because it tapered dramatically beneath my ribs, then flared out again to my hips —an hourglass, my mother had said with a smile, defining it for me.

She told me I should be proud of my healthy shape and healthy body, and love and treasure it because it was mine. No one, she said, could tell me what to think of my body. If I let another person's opinion matter I was giving him or her control over me, and I had complete control over my self-image.

That's what she said.

But that wasn't the truth, not really. Because even though I knew Ben was a bottom feeder of the worst sort and his opinion mattered just as much as the coruscations in the sea, words like *fatty* hurt, no matter the source.

I felt Martin's eyes on me and I wished I had a shirt, a bathrobe, or a big plastic trash bag to cover the imperfections of my shape. Furthermore, I wished I'd junk punched Ben when I'd had the chance.

Martin moved, walking on Sam's towel and sitting next to me. I lifted my chin and kept my eyes on the horizon; I was not yet ready to look at him. I was still trying to gain control of my scattered feelings. I was also attempting to suppress the self-consciousness creeping from my chest to my throat and choking me. I was this awkward, pudgy girl, the color of chalk, sitting alongside a muscled and bronzed Greek god.

Martin stretched his long legs in front of him; he rested a hand behind me so his arm and chest brushed against the bare skin of my arm and back. The contact was a spark in my tunnel of frigid numbness. Then he leaned forward, nuzzled my cheek softly with his nose, and placed a gentle kiss on my jaw. Unexpectedly, I felt myself melt.

"Hey, Parker," he whispered, then kissed the hollow of my cheek. "What's wrong?"

I shook my head even as my body instinctively leaned into him, my shoulder resting against his chest. He felt good, solid, warm.

"Why is that guy here?" I asked.

Martin glanced over his shoulder to where his teammates were eating, then faced me again. "Did he say something to you?"

I cleared my throat then answered with another question, "Why would you invite him? After what he tried to do to you."

He exhaled softly, then brushed the back of his fingers down the length of my arm to my elbow; his eyes followed the path. He seemed to be studying my hand where it gripped my leg.

"Because he's strong and we, the boat, need him to win." His voice held an edge of ire, but I knew it wasn't directed at me.

I slid my eyes to the side, considered this news and Martin's expression. He didn't look happy about having Ben there. In fact, he looked angrily resigned. I got the impression he wasn't used to making compromises, and this one felt wrong and unwieldy.

"He tried to drug you," I stated with a fervor that surprised me, feeling outraged on Martin's behalf.

"I didn't say I trust him. I said we *need* him. Trusting and needing someone are usually mutually exclusive." Martin lifted his dazzling eyes to mine. This close I was startled to see they were the exact color of the ocean. Flecks of green, silver, and turquoise radiated from his pupil like a starburst.

"But sometimes, rarely…," he started, stopped, his attention drifting to my lips briefly, "you meet someone you need, who you can also trust."

He stared at me and I stared back, feeling muddled and disbelieving the implication of his words. He allowed me to struggle for a full minute, then he reached for my hand and pried it from my leg, holding it lightly, reverently.

"Kaitlyn, did Ben say something to you? Because if he did I'll get rid of him." Martin's eyes narrowed by a fraction and his gaze grew penetrating, searching.

I gathered an expansive breath and turned from Martin's probing stare. His obvious concern was doing strange things to me. His protectiveness didn't feel like possessiveness, and I wondered how often I'd lamentably mistaken one for the other.

I didn't want to lie. But if Martin could live with Ben trying to drug and extort him for the sake of team cohesion, then I guess I could live with a few nasty words.

Of course, there was the whole Ben drugging girls for undefined reasons issue...

I looked over the water as I spoke. "Martin, I didn't tell you this on Friday when I saw you at the party, but you're not the first person Ben has tried to drug. When he was talking to that girl, he made it sound like…like he's been drugging girls for a while. That can really only mean one thing, right?"

I peeked at Martin and his scowl was fierce. He said through gritted teeth, "Thanks for letting me know. I'll handle Ben. He won't—" he stopped, exhaled slowly, "he won't be doing that again."

"But what about what he's done so far?"

"I'll take care of that too."

"He's so awful. He's…he's like ammonium dichromate with mercury thiocyanate. He's the college boy equivalent of the bowels of hell."

Martin's smile was sudden and its unexpectedness seemed to take us both by surprise; he laughed lightly at my analogy, but he also looked concerned. "Hey, did he say something to you? Before I came over?"

"I don't like him," I said, then rushed on when I feared Martin would see I was being evasive. "He's unpleasant and creepy and I don't want to talk about him anymore. Let's talk about chemistry."

I felt rather than saw Martin's small smile because he'd leaned forward and nipped my shoulder, his lips hovering against my skin. "Yes, let's talk about chemistry. We have excellent chemistry."

I leaned a tad to the side and away because his soft lips, sharp teeth, and hot mouth were overwhelming to my chest, stomach, and pants.

"I meant our assignment. I brought all my notes, I think we should start on the literature search this afternoon."

"Na-ah." Martin lifted his head, placed my hand on his thigh, and then gathered several stray strands of hair away from my face. He tucked them behind my ear. "We're leaving. You and I have plans."

"Plans? What plans?"

"I know a place where we can be alone."

"Other than the fifty spare rooms back at the house?" I said, then immediately felt myself burn scarlet at the unintended insinuation. "Ah…I mean…that is…what I mean is…oh blast it."

He watched me struggle under his suspended eyebrows, a whisper of a smile on his face, then cut in when I tried to hide my face in my arm. "No, the place I have in mind is better. Lunch is packed. Come on." He squeezed my arm then pulled my hand as he stood, tugging me with him. "We need to get going."

I snatched my hand back and quickly covered myself with a towel.

I tried not to look at him, mostly because he was magnificent. Unlike the others, he was clothed in board shorts that ended at his knee. His shirtless torso was flawless and completely smooth. He looked like a golden statue, cast in hard relief by the sun, but warm to the touch. And that was just his torso! I didn't trust my gaze to venture downward to assess the flawlessness of his legs...or elsewhere.

My heart and the area previously defined as "my pants" both twisted and tightened at the sight of his perfect body. I felt pinpricks and tingles all over and a little lightheaded as I turned away from him.

"Let me get changed first," I mumbled without thinking. "I wish I'd invested in a burqa or a moomoo..."

Martin gripped the towel as I tried to wrap it under my arms, bringing my attention back to him.

His expression was again fierce, his eyebrows lowered in a frowny scowl. "What did you say?"

"Nothing."

"What are you doing?" His gaze flickered to the towel then back to mine.

"Getting my things."

He yanked on the towel and I held it tighter. His frown intensified. As he surveyed my face, I felt very much like I was being examined under a microscope.

Martin took three full, measured breaths, his hand now stubbornly fisted in the terrycloth, before he asked again through clenched teeth, "What did Ben say to you, Parker?"

"Nothing important." I tilted my chin upward and shrugged. When he looked like he was going to press the issue further, I let go of the towel, letting the weight of it drop in his grip.

Martin looked troubled, but his attention strayed as though he were compelled, as though he had no choice but to look at my body. I tensed, fought the urge to cross my arms over my chest, and glanced at the sky, letting him look.

It didn't really matter. We were at the beach for Bunsen's sake! Sooner or later he was going to see me in a bathing suit. I repeated my mother's sage advice, *If I let another person's opinion matter then I was giving him control over me; I alone had complete control over my self-image.* I held still for as long as I could.

Then I heard him sigh. "Fuck me..."

My eyes darted back to Martin and I found him looking at my body with a mixture of pained hunger and appreciation. The profanity had slipped from his tongue like an odd caress.

"Excuse me?" I questioned, though I almost asked, *Was that a request?*

His gaze jumped to my face and he stepped forward, tossing the towel to the sand. He didn't touch me except to fit the fingers of my left hand in the palm of his right. "It's an expression, Parker. It usually means a person is surprised."

I squinted at him. "What's surprising? Is it my ghost-like skin? Does it scare you?"

I saw his mouth tugged to the side just before he turned from me and pulled me toward the house path. "No. Your ghost skin doesn't scare me."

"Is it—"

"You're fucking, goddamn gorgeous, Parker," he said roughly, a half growl, and without looking back at me.

Startled, I snapped my mouth shut, as a pleased and pleasant warmth suffused my cheeks, chest, and stomach. For the first time in my life I found I didn't mind the use of curse words.

[9]
REACTIONS IN AQUEOUS SOLUTION

I DIDN'T CHANGE clothes as I completely forgot that I wanted to change clothes. Therefore I continued to wear my relatively modest, halter-top, two-piece bathing suit on the ride from the house to this new and better place where Martin insisted we go…to be alone…

Being alone with Martin didn't freak me out at first. It felt like a very theoretical state of being; like being informed I was going to go become quark–gluon plasma (i.e. one of the theoretical phases of matter) or the winning contestant on American Idol. So, equally likely.

The truth was that my mind was slow on the uptake because everything was happening too fast. On Friday afternoon I was hiding in a science cabinet on campus. It was now Sunday afternoon and Martin was practically wooing me—insomuch as crazy handsome, billionaire, geniuses woo a girl—on a small island in the Caribbean.

I was not used to change and I was not good with surprises. The entirety of my past and all changes therein were well documented via the agendas prepared by George. I'd always had time to prepare.

But not this time.

Thus, I forgot to freak out until he was leading me by the hand down a sandy path and through a healthy amount of tropical underbrush. In his other hand he held a picnic basket. I glanced up and blinked at the broad muscles of his back and it abruptly hit me where I was and who I was with and what we'd done so far.

The kissing, the touching, the whispering, the shared moments *and* the heated stares. I'd made eye contact with him more in the last thirty-six hours than I had in the last six months as his lab partner. A shiver passed through me. Life was happening too fast.

I mumbled, "Fast, quick, rapid, supersonic, hurried…"

Martin glanced over his shoulder, his oceanic eyes sweeping me up and down. "What did you say?"

"Nothing."

His eyes narrowed on me. "Are you okay?"

I lied, "Yes. Good." Then deflected, "Where are we going?"

A glint of some devilry flashed in his gaze, curving his mouth to one side—devilry looked really good on Martin Sandeke—and he returned his attention to the path. "Just this place I know with a water-fall and cave. It's part of the estate, so no one else uses it."

"How nice," I said, bending as he held a palm frond out of my way, and added conversationally, "we have a garage at my house. It holds a car and some of my dad's tools."

Martin glanced at me, equal parts amused and confused. "Oh?"

"Yes. And a hammock in the back yard."

"Is that so…"

"Yeah."

"So, no waterfalls?"

"No. But this one time, when it rained a lot, the gutter broke. That was similar to a waterfall."

Martin laughed. I knew he was laughing because, though he was quiet, I saw his shoulders shake; and when he turned to look at me, his eyes were bright with humor and he was flashing a lethally bright smile.

"You're funny, Parker."

"Thank you." I looked away from the beacon of his smile. It was blinding. "You're also…humorous at times."

We walked another hundred yards or so in silence and I forced myself to study the surrounding landscape. The ground was sandy—

light grey and white—and heavily littered with bleached shells. Tall palm trees provided the ceiling of the canopy. The path was littered with thick palm bushes and underbrush. All around us insects buzzed and hummed a constant symphony, and I could make out the faint sounds of rushing water. It grew louder the farther we walked but not overwhelming. The weather was warm, and would have been hot if we were in the sun and farther inland. But in the shade and so near the ocean, a cool breeze whispered over and cooled my bare skin.

Martin turned slightly, still holding my hand, though his attention was on a series of rocks before us that descended a stairway of sorts.

"Be careful here, just watch your step. It might be better if you do this barefoot. You're not going to need shoes anyway."

He released my hand, kicked off his shoes, and preceded me down the path made by the sandy boulders.

I, likewise, kicked off my flip flops and followed, keeping my attention on the trail. The sound of the rushing water increased exponentially as we descended. Then I stopped because Martin stopped, and I looked up and saw this place where he'd brought us.

And my mouth fell open.

He'd brought us to a very small cove, mostly shaded by palms and the surrounding rock face. It was about twenty feet in diameter. The crystal clear, turquoise water was mostly still, but rippled near the far end. Upon closer inspection, the cove appeared to be adjacent to a cave. The waterfall was unseen, but I heard it; I guess it must be behind the rock face.

It was like a little room, private, intimate, breathtaking.

I don't know exactly how long I stood there gaping at the small natural loveliness of our surroundings. But I became aware of Martin's gaze all at once, watching me; I darted a look at him, snapping my mouth shut.

"Do you like it?"

I nodded. "It's…it's stunning."

He grinned, obviously pleased. He'd set the picnic basket down at some point on a shelf created by the curving rocks, leaving both of his hands free. Martin with two hands free felt a little dangerous. I glanced at his hands, my heart skipping.

"Come on," he said, holding one of his dangerous hands out to me.

I accepted it, and he led us down into the water, his eyes holding mine. It lapped at my ankle, then calf, then we were submerged to our waists just three feet from the edge.

"How deep is this?"

"Uh, that's an entrance to the cave where the waterfall is." He indicated with his head to the far side. "It's relatively deep over there, maybe fifteen or twenty feet. But on this side," he pointed to my right, "it's flat and about three or four feet."

"Have you gone into the cave?"

He nodded, his eyes traveling over me. It was a slow perusal of my body that did things, unexpected things, like made me tremble, my stomach flip, and my nipples harden. The longer he stared the hotter and more intense his gaze grew. It felt like he was on the precipice of something, saying something.

I didn't want him jumping off any verbal cliffs, so I interrupted him, pulling my hand from his, before he could speak. "What's the plan, Stan? What's the deal, Neil? Is there a schedule for the rest of this week? Anything I should be aware of? I remind you again and in all seriousness that I have two papers to write and a vector calculus test to study for. Also, again, you and I do have that lab assignment we need to prep. I have you trapped here, therefore I expect you to help with the literature search. Also, I have two books I've been dying to read."

Martin wasn't smiling, but his eyes were warm and interested. "Do you always talk like that?"

"Like what? Like awesome?"

"Yeah, like awesome." His tone was serious, verging on earnest.

I felt pleased by the compliment despite the fact I'd self-deprecatingly complimented myself and he'd merely agreed. Because I did want to be his friend so it was important to be honest. "Actually, no. Truthfully, you make me nervous so I'm a little more jumpy and vociferous than usual."

"Vociferous. You have an excellent vocabulary." He pushed

himself backward a few feet and began treading water near the center of the cove. His eyes seemed to glow, reflecting the sea-green of the saltwater.

"Ah, yes. That I do. I'm a big fan of synonyms."

He exhaled a soft laugh, peering at me like I was weird and wonderful. It made my smile widen.

"So, plan for this week? What can I expect?" I took small steps near the edge, not wanting to venture too close to Martin and his glowing eyes and dangerous hands.

"Well, team practice, like this morning. The waves are minimal on this side of the island because we're basically set in the middle of a large inlet. The Gulf is like a big lake. We'll be practicing and training in the mornings, so you'll get your quiet time." His voice was downright conversational. It was nice.

"Good." I tucked my hair behind my ears, this news settled my nerves somewhat. If he was training in the mornings then I could use the time to prepare my friend attacks.

"But in the afternoons and evenings...," he paused, licked his lips, his eyes flickering over me, "I want us to be together."

This news halted my progress around the rim of the cove. Paired with the predatory glint in his eyes and the slight undercurrent of a mandate in his words, my insides felt like a jumble of knots...made out of magma. That's right, magma knots. Perhaps if I hadn't skipped breakfast my stomach wouldn't have been so tumultuous.

"To have tacos?" Despite my best efforts, this question emerged somewhat high-pitched and breathless.

"Yes, tacos. And there will be parties and other things."

Parties.

Parties?

What?

I frowned. I'm pretty sure I scowled. This reaction was instinctual. I hated parties. Hate.

"Parties?" I may have curled my lip in a miniature sneer.

"Yeah, on the island, at some of the other houses, friends of mine. You know, the usual college scene stuff."

Usual college scene...just a bunch of billionaires' kids and their friends. It sounded delightful.

"Yeah, no thanks." I pulled my eyes from his, inspected the rocks. "I don't go to parties. It's one of my life rules."

"Life rules?"

"Yes. Good ideas to live by."

"You just made that up. Not going to parties isn't one of your life rules."

He was right, I had just made up not going to parties as a life rule, but he didn't need to know that. Therefore I ignored his last comment and tried to act blasé. "I don't want to go, but don't let that stop you from going."

"Parker."

I sighed, then met his gaze.

"I want you to come."

"No, thank you."

He ground his teeth. "Kaitlyn, you promised you were going to give this a try."

"I will..."

Once again he was giving me the severe stare down, likely because my weakly delivered *I will* didn't even sound convincing to me.

Managing to swallow around the sudden thickness in my throat, I squared my shoulders so I was facing him.

"Here's the thing, Sandeke. I am. I am going to give this a try. Despite my worries—"

"What worries?" He sounded exasperated.

I ignored his question. "Despite my worries and reservations, I'm going to give this the good college try. But I don't even know how to dance. I can tango like a pro, but I don't do the body wiggle weird thing. And isn't that what the kids do these days at parties? Dance?"

He lifted an eyebrow at my excuse—obviously unimpressed—and with two fluid strokes moved to join me.

I stiffened, my eyes wide, and backed up a step at his advance. "What...what are you doing?"

"I'm going to teach you how to dance," he said simply, already on me, reaching for my body.

I stiffened further, feeling unaccountably breathless as his big hands slipped around my waist and settled on my hips and lower back.

"But there…but we…but—"

"Shhh," he said, pulling me closer. "Relax."

"Create cold fusion," I murmured in response, unable to relax and placing my hands nowhere, because placing them anywhere on Martin felt perilous to my well-being.

He glanced down at me, his eyebrows in a perplexed V. "What does cold fusion have to do with anything?"

"You tell me to relax, which is impossible. I tell you to create cold fusion, which is impossible."

His answering smile was crooked. "You can't relax?"

"No."

"Why not?"

"You know why not."

"Well, it might help if you touched me."

"That will not help."

"It might."

"It won't."

"Touch me."

I scowled at his chest, my hands still in the air at my sides. *Stupid perfect chest.*

"Parker, if we're going to dance you have to touch me." He sounded amused and his fingers flexed on my bare skin. I felt the roughened calluses of his palms just before he released my body to grab my hands. He brought them to his shoulders, pressed them there, then returned his own to my hips. I didn't miss the fact that his hand placement was now a bit more daring than it had been a moment ago, lower, closer to my bottom.

I swallowed thickly, glaring at my fingers where they touched his perfectly sculpted shoulder.

"Don't you want to touch me?" he asked, his inflection daring, teasing, but also something else. Something hesitant and uncertain.

I lifted my eyes to his; they were guarded, his smile looked bracing, almost like a grimace, like he was preparing himself for bad news.

I sighed. I knew I sounded resigned and a little pitiful. "Yes…"

His gaze thawed as it dropped to my lips. "Then you should… because I want you to."

"I don't know how," I blurted.

"I'll teach you." His voice was low, soft, and held a promise.

"I'm not good at this."

"We haven't even started."

"I don't mean the dancing, I mean the touching. I'm pretty sure I'll be good at the wiggle dancing once I apply myself, as I have excellent rhythm." Heat was beginning to build in the space between us where we didn't touch; my stomach and his, his chest and mine. I had the sudden sensation we were magnetized, and I had to make my body rigid to keep from plastering myself against him.

"Why do you think you'll be good at dancing? You're very stiff, you need to loosen up." He swayed his hips and mine to the left, then the right, then back, his movements measured and slow. I moved with him, trying to loosen up without succumbing to the magnetism.

"Because I used to ballroom dance and I play three instruments. Did you know that? And also the drums…so I guess four instruments."

His eyes, which were still on my lips, flickered to mine and his eyebrows ticked upward with surprise. "Really? What else do you play?" He sounded interested.

"Guitar mostly. But also the piano and saxophone and the aforementioned drums."

He smiled. I swear he'd been smiling so much it felt unnatural. Before now, I thought I'd seen him smile three times in the last six months and all three of those times the smile had been mean and hard because he'd been about to unleash a world of hurt on someone.

These were different smiles, relaxed and happy smiles. They were devastating and no less precarious to my wellbeing than his mean and hard smiles.

"I'd like to see that," he said after a beat. "I'd like to see you play."

"We can go back now and I'll show you. I think I saw a guitar in one of the rooms back at *the compound.*" I said "the compound" in a deep, weird voice, hoping to cut through the raging tension building between us, making it difficult for me to breathe.

I made like I was going to move away. His grip on me tightened, staying my attempted retreat.

"No." He shook his head, the word sharp, and his eyes flashed with a warning. Then he brought me flush against him.

This was not a good idea. It drove all the breath from my lungs and I trembled, gasped, spikes of hot and cold rushing under the surface of my skin. I felt sensitized everywhere. Instinctively, my eyes shut, startled by the ferocity of the sensual, swirling, damning, overwhelming physical feels.

He half growled, half groaned then set me away, placing essential distance between us. My lashes fluttered open and I found him watching me with his jaw set and his eyes ablaze. His hands were on his hips and I saw his Adam's apple move with a thick swallow.

I shifted on my feet, not sure what to do with my arms. I decided to place them in the water at my sides. "Sorry."

"Why are you sorry?"

"I don't know. I guess I'm not sorry."

He growled, his eyes half closing, and he tugged a hand through his hair. He looked…frustrated.

His frustration made me frustrated because I didn't know why he was frustrated. I surmised based on his expression that I'd done something wrong, made some novice misstep, but I had no idea what.

I hated I was so clueless about boys. I didn't know anything about them other than what one can absorb from porn and pubmed articles. Otherwise they were a cornucopia of conundrums.

"What's going on?" I blurted, feeling lost and confused by the last sixty seconds, not to mention the last two days. My hands convulsively gripped my thighs in the water. "What are you thinking?"

His eyes lifted to mine and he stared at me, saying nothing, but his frustration was tangible. I could hear him breathe though, could see his chest rise and fall with his deep exhales. The longer he stared at me without saying anything the faster my heart beat; I felt like it was going to throw itself out of my ribcage.

Then he said, "Come here," causing me to jump a little, though his voice was quiet, almost lost amidst the combined sounds of the waterfall and the insect symphony. Even if I hadn't heard the words, I would have read the want—what *he* wanted—in his eyes. He looked a little wild with want.

I tried to take a deep breath but managed only a shallow inhale. Silently I obeyed, wading toward him until a foot separated us. I was glad my hands were in the water so he couldn't see them shaking, because they were shaking—just a little.

When I stopped, his gaze dropped to my body, to my chest, ribs, and stomach. My lower belly felt tight and my breasts heavy. Full. The force of his stare was physical—corporeal—and I shifted a half step backward under its intensity.

Maybe he thought I was going to turn and flee, or maybe he'd reached the limit of his patience. Whatever the reason, Martin closed the remaining distance between us. He gripped my waist again. This time the shock of sensation from Martin's rough calluses against my bare midriff sent a jolt to my center and up to my heart.

He held me firmly as though he didn't trust me to stay.

"I need to touch you."

"You are touching me," I whispered breathlessly, unable to tear my gaze from his.

Martin shook his head slowly, lifted one hand to the tie at my neck that was holding up my top. Without breaking eye contact, he tugged on the fastening, loosening, then releasing the halter. With a featherlight touch he brought the straps forward, the tips of his fingers on my neck and shoulder sending a shiver down my spine. His movements were slow and purposeful, and he didn't stop pulling, and his eyes never left mine.

He brought his other hand to the second strap, the backs of his knuckles brushing against the tops of my breasts—pulling, pulling, still pulling—until he delved with meticulously measured movements into the material of my bikini top and tugged it down with aching deliberateness, exposing my body.

His gaze dropped to my bare breasts and he blinked, his eyes half lidded, the rise and fall of his chest obvious.

Then he touched me with the backs of his hands and knuckles—my hardened nipples and the undersides of my breasts—until the top was lowered completely. My stomach twisted and my back arched on instinct. I was near panting now.

I felt crazed, overwhelmed, like I was on the precipice of a high cliff and needed to jump—I had to. I had no choice. I absolutely needed it. Whatever Martin was about to do, I needed it.

A small, helpless sound escaped my lips, something like a whimper, causing his gaze to sharpen and his body to sway toward mine. I realized his chest was rising and falling faster than it had been, and the sense he was close to a similar edge made me bold.

So I touched him.

It was just my fingertips against the hard ridges of his abdomen, but it made him flinch and release a growly sigh like I'd both hurt and pleased him.

"Kaitlyn…" My name from his lips was tight, choked, needy.

He shifted an inch closer; the water swirled around us. One of his hands slid back up my body and cupped me—reverently at first, like I was fragile—and his other moved lower, around my back, slipping into the fabric of my boy short bikini bottoms, inside, down, until he was gripping my bare ass with one hand and massaging my breast with the other, his thumb sweeping over the peak twice before pinching it.

I cried out, the spike of pleasure severe and unexpected and clearly wired straight to my core. My hands instinctively lifted to grip his shoulders and my back flexed, arching on instinct.

"Dammit." His eyes half closed, and he brought me against him with a jerky movement, as though it were a reflex he couldn't control.

Suddenly he bent at his waist and his mouth was on me. He licked, kissed, and sucked my nipple into his hot mouth, then grazed it with his teeth.

"Ah! Martin." My eyes drifted shut briefly and my hips bucked, my grip on his shoulders increasing. I felt taut and swollen and greedy for his touch, his hands, his mouth, his body.

"I have to touch you." His voice rumbled. He circled the center of my breast with his tongue before drawing it between his lips.

"You are touching me," I repeated, holding on to his neck and the back of his head, pressing him to my chest, and feeling a little insane.

"Not here," he growled, his caresses growing more aggressive, insistent, forceful.

He bit the underside of my breast and my ribs like he wanted to consume me, his fingers on my bottom digging into my flesh, severe and punishing. He pinched my nipple again, this time harder, and it hurt, but it also felt necessary. Then his hand in my bikini moved from my bottom to my front, his fingers parting and entering me.

Martin straightened, then captured my lips with his just as I cried out my surprise. His tongue mirrored the stroking of his fingers. His free hand grabbed my ponytail and he roughly positioned me how he liked, tilting my head to the side, opening my mouth just as he was opening my center.

My nipples grazed his chest. I flexed my thighs, my stomach, and my back tight. My nails dug into his shoulders and back. His fingers were inside me and it wasn't the soft teasing he'd employed in my dorm room. This was rough, urgent, his fingers searching, uncomfortable and a little painful, but...God, it felt so good. So good. So, so good.

My body seemed to understand what my mind hadn't yet discovered and my hips rocked instinctively in time with his strokes. He bit my lip as I panted, his hot mouth moving to my jaw then neck as he yanked my hair, exposing the vulnerable expanse of skin to his teeth and tongue.

As though from a great distance, I heard him cussing and complimenting me. A steady stream of growled *fucks* and *beautifuls* and *gorgeous* and *damns* between clenched teeth, against my skin, hot breath spilling over my ear and neck. I became aware all at once that his erection was pressed against my hip and he was moving the hard length, rubbing against me, as I moved on his hand. My breath hitched as my stomach coiled tight. My jaw was tight. Everything felt tight and taut and close to breaking.

And then I did.

I broke.

In fact, I cried out.

Violent, sweet desolation tore through me, delicious spasms accompanied by fierce trembling. I was paralyzed by this vicious wave of beautiful destruction, strangling and releasing and suffocating me over and over. I became aware of his fingers stroking slower, softer, like they'd taken what they wanted and were now moving as a mere echo of their earlier urgency.

My body also instinctively relaxed without my telling it to do so, going almost limp. Martin's mouth was on my neck, sucking, licking, and biting. I felt his heart beating against my bare breast and its thunderous pace matched mine. My vision was blurry and I realized I wasn't breathing, so I gasped for air, swallowing a gasping breath as I buried my face below his neck, hiding.

I felt him shudder. His fingers inside my body, still stroking and petting—like I'd done something good and he was rewarding me with a gentle touch.

With plain reluctance, he slipped his hand from my bikini shorts and released my pony tail. At first I thought he was going to set me away again, but he didn't. He embraced me. His strong arms came around my body and he crushed me to him. Automatically I snuggled closer.

I wasn't confused. I was nothing other than my body. Blissfully satiated. My mind was completely blank, devoid of thought. I merely felt.

And everything about being in Martin's arms felt like bliss.

[10]
PROPERTIES OF SOLUTIONS

Once again, Sam and I took dinner in my room.

It took me a while to recover from…

MY VERY FIRST ORGASM!!!

That's how I thought about it in my brain.

MY VERY FIRST ORGASM!!!!!!!!

It was all capital letters, followed by a ridiculous number of exclamation points. In the past I'd tried to bring myself to satisfaction any number of times and always failed, which was why I'd done so much research about the sex act. I thought if I could read enough about the subject I would eventually find the key to…wait for it…

MY VERY FIRST ORGASM!!!!!!!!!!!!

I didn't expect it to render me speechless, but it did, and for several hours. Luckily and bewilderingly, Martin also seemed to require recovery time. Neither of us spoke afterward, not in the cove, not on the walk back to the golf cart, not on the ride back to the estate.

Although, some barrier between us had been shattered, because he seemed to feel at liberty to kiss me and touch me whenever and however he wanted, and I let him because I quite simply needed the post-orgasm reassurance and touching. It felt necessary and natural and I craved it.

Before wordlessly retying my halter, he lavished my breasts and shoulders with hot, wet kisses—fondling my body like it was his with which to play and explore as he liked. As we left the cove, he pulled me into his arms and kissed me until I was climbing him breathlessly. During the duration of the drive in the golf cart, he placed one possessive hand on my thigh, then caressed my bottom greedily as we walked to the house.

Once inside, he caught my hand and spun me around until we were pressed against each other from knees to chests, and he kissed me again, his hands smoothing down my neck, then shoulders, arms, waist, and hips.

When we finally separated, he wore a deeply satisfied smile and his eyes glowed like they had in the cove.

Then he spoke. "Go clean up. Take this."

I glanced down at the basket he was holding. It was the picnic we hadn't eaten. I took it then returned my gaze to his.

"You should eat something," he said.

I nodded obediently.

His smile grew. "Are you ever going to speak again?"

I blinked at him then shrugged my *I don't know*.

Speak? Speak? What was that?

He laughed, pulled me in for another hug, and kissed the top of my head. His eyes were happy as he sent me on my way with a low, "See you at dinner."

But I didn't see him at dinner. I ate in my room with Sam because my mind caught up with what had happened while I took my shower. I felt the soreness between my legs and reality crashed over me like a tempestuous waterfall. The world came into sharp focus. I reached for the wall of the shower to steady myself.

His fingers hadn't been gentle, hence the soreness. And as I reflected on the events in the cove, I recognized that everything about him—his touch, his words, his kisses—had been dictatorial, forceful, and domineering. He may have given me my very first orgasm, but he'd taken something as well.

And he knew it. He'd known it *while* it was happening.

Adding to my confused state, I saw in the bathroom mirror that he'd left bite marks and hickies on my skin - two on my neck, and one on the underside of my right breast. They looked like evidence. Like they'd been placed there purposefully.

I needed time to marinate in the events, to accept it had happened, to decide what it meant, to figure out why I'd let it happen, and to determine whether it was a good thing or a bad thing.

I didn't panic. But I did remember that the blood of a thousand virgins had been sacrificed at the altar of his sexual prowess.

A cold lump gathered in my stomach, comprised of confusion and uneasiness, and I dressed in sweatpants and a large T-shirt.

Sam stopped by about an hour later—found me curled on my giant bed staring out the window to the sea. Though I knew she noticed the purple marks on my neck, she seemed to sense I didn't want to talk, and I was grateful when she suggested we eat dinner then study in my room. I'd brought my class-specific notebooks, to which I had an unhealthy attachment, therefore I was all for getting down to study town.

My notebooks were soothing to me. Just seeing my hand-written notes was like going back in time to the day of the lecture. They gave me confidence. They made me feel like I might actually be capable of acing tests. They were the brain-spinach to my Popeye the sailor man.

As well, I didn't really want to face Martin's teammates with hickies, obvious evidence of what we'd done. I wasn't regretful or embarrassed, but it felt private, sacred to me. I didn't want to share what had transpired with a room full of near strangers, especially with Ben the leering douche-bucket.

Therefore, Sam and I sat on the balcony and munched on salmon cakes, garden salad, and asparagus, between chapters and class notes of vector calculus and European history. At sunset we went for a walk on the beach. She told me about her day, wherein she swam with Eric then convinced him to play tennis with her.

Of course she kicked his ass.

I didn't ask her whether she liked him and she didn't ask me what was going on with Martin. In a lot of ways Sam and I were similar.

When real, weighty feelings were involved, we both found vocalizing unformed thoughts difficult. I think we both needed time to figure out our own stuff before talking it through with each other.

During our walk we decided to share my giant bed again, so she went off in search of her PJs, while I grabbed the tray with our dirty dishes and wandered around the house in search of the kitchen. I needed tea, not to mention cookies.

In the kitchen I encountered the chef—a red-cheeked, red-haired, red-nosed woman in her sixties named Irma, and her aide—a similarly red-cheeked, red-haired, red-nosed forty-something woman, Tamra— who I suspected was Irma's daughter. They gently admonished me for clearing my own dishes then promised to bring me up tea, milk, and cookies. I asked for directions back to my room, and Tamra offered to show me the way.

Upon my request, she was showing me the most direct path, rather than the scenic route, as I suspected I would make several stealthy trips to the kitchen during my stay. I probed her for answers about the house as we walked, and learned it had been acquired by Mr. Sandeke senior —Martin's father—ten or so years ago. The staff came with the house. I also learned Tamra was divorced and childless, and had moved down to work with her mother some four years prior.

They lived at the house in staff quarters year round and fed the rest of the staff daily—most of whom were also employed year round. However, Mr. Thompson and Mrs. Greenstone were also responsible for several other extensive family properties in England, Italy, Switzerland, Thailand, Japan, New Zealand, and the United States. They traveled with the family and always opened the houses for Martin and his parents wherever they went.

We turned into the long hallway that led to my suite when Tamra stopped—walking and talking—suddenly, then took a step back.

"Oh! Mr. Sandeke." Tamra turned toward me, gave me a tight smile, then walked off without another word.

I watched her go, a bit perplexed by how suddenly she fled her employer.

When I turned back to my door I understood why. Martin's eyes were deep blue pools of unhappiness and his jaw was set in a firm, grim line.

"Where have you been?"

My eyebrows ticked upward—because his demanding question made me want to junk punch him—then lowered—because I remembered he now had carnal knowledge of me and I'd not joined him for dinner like we'd agreed.

Also, despite his grumpy tone and face, my body apparently wanted him to give me the rough treatment again, because it melted and hummed under his scowl of dissatisfaction.

I straightened my spine, giving my body a mental slap aimed at sobriety, and lifted my chin.

I was careful to keep my voice nice and steady. "I've been cavorting with the servants."

"Cavorting," he repeated, his tone flat. But I was pleased to see the granite-like edge to his jaw soften and his eyes lose their harsh glint.

"Yes. Cavorting for cookies. I wandered the halls for a while, got lost, then eventually found the kitchen." I said this while walking toward him as casually as I was able, then entered my room, leaving the door open behind me in a silent invitation.

He took the invite and closed the door as he followed. I heard him sigh before he demanded, "Why weren't you at dinner?"

"Sam and I decided to get some studying done. And I was tired." I crossed to the sitting area by the big window and plopped down in a chair, then gave him a small, friendly smile. "How are the boys? Quite recovered from the perils of traveling via private plane, limo and yacht, and practice this morning?"

Some of the sharpness re-entered his gaze and he crossed his arms over his chest. "You would prefer to fly commercial?"

"Of course not. I'd prefer not to fly at all. I insist you teleport me the next time we take a vacation to paradise."

He finally cracked a smile and crossed to where I sat. He examined me for a moment in silence, then took the chair next to mine. He eased into it, all fluid grace, long limbs, and coiled power.

"The next time?" he asked, and I was pleased to hear his voice held a hint of teasing.

"Of course. I've decided that you and I are going to be best friends, just as long as you keep me in a steady supply of salmon cakes."

"And cookies."

"Yes. And cookies." I bent my elbow on the high, cushioned arm of the chair and rested my cheek against my hand, let my eyes move over his handsome features and found him watching me, his eyes intent.

His mouth curved into a smirk that was mirrored in his stare. "And dancing lessons?"

I grew very still, my eyes locked on his, because by dancing lessons, I knew he meant orgasms. Probably mutual orgasms. And lots of them.

I swallowed thickly, and heat traveled up my chest to my neck. The cold lump in my stomach seemed to balloon and press against my lungs. I thought about the marks on my skin and the soreness between my legs, reminders of how physical intimacy with Martin had been exciting and satisfying, but also extremely intense and a little scary. Maybe too intense.

He reached for my hand where it rested against my cheek and I stiffened, straightened, and yanked it away, opting instead to twist my fingers together on my lap. I also tore my gaze from his and stared at the floor.

We were silent for a stretch as I tried to figure out what to say, how to respond. This was problematic as I didn't know what to say or how to respond.

"Look at me."

I tried to swallow again but experienced a swallow misfire, and released a shaky breath. "Martin…" I covered my face with my hands. My cheeks were hot and I shook my head.

"Kaitlyn, if you tell me you regret what happened…" His voice was low, sounded tight and barely controlled.

"I don't regret it," I blurted, because it was true. I didn't regret it. I liked it, a lot. And I wanted to do it again.

I peered at him from between my fingers, found him watching me, his jaw set and his eyes fierce. When I spoke it was muffled by my palms pressed to my mouth. "I don't regret it. But I don't know how to feel about it because it was a little scary."

His gaze grew introspective, like he was searching his memory, and I noted his forehead was marred with wrinkles of concern. "Scary? How so?"

I tried to distance myself from the conversation and approach it with pragmatic analysis. "Well, I think the first true 'sexual experience' for any girl is going to be frightening, so there is that. But also... well...I'm sore. And you left bruises on my hip and bites on my neck. You were quite intense and I liked that a lot, but you weren't very...gentle."

He blinked rapidly and a flicker of something like dismay clouded his features. He studied me with pensive unhappiness. Then his head fell backward to the cushion of the chair and his chest expanded with a large breath. "Goddammit."

He looked angry.

"Are you...mad?" I asked, my hands dropping to my lap as I studied his face for a clue. I couldn't believe he was angry. For heaven's sake, I was new at this, at *all* of this.

He closed his eyes for a full five seconds, then said, "I didn't mean to hurt you, not at all. I don't *want* to hurt you."

I examined him, how upset he was, and realized that irritation was pointed inward. "Can you be—I mean—is it possible for you to be less rough?"

He lifted his head, his eyes opening and I saw his determination before he spoke. "Yes. You have my word. That won't happen again."

I got the sense he was disappointed in himself...*very curious.*

"I didn't say that exactly. I mean," I cleared my throat, trying to quash my nervousness, because it was weird doing a post-orgasm analysis with Martin Sandeke, "so, just to be clear, it was good. It was all *very good.* I liked what happened...earlier. My pants liked it too. But, as much as my pants want to get this party started, I'm very new to all of this." I emphasized *all of this* by waving my hands over my pelvis then waving them in the direction of his entire body.

Some of his dismay gave way to amusement. "I know."

"I'm not saying the rough was bad, and I'm not ruling it out for future interludes—if there are future interludes—as long as I get to be rough sometimes too."

His gaze abruptly heated and his eyes narrowed, sharpened. I ignored this because the idea of getting rough with Martin was... epically arousing. I rushed to continue, "I'm just suggesting that, if this happens again—"

"When it happens again."

"—you go a little easier on me until I know how to do this thing."

He nodded and I was pleased to see him relax a bit more.

We stared at each other for a beat, and the air felt ripe and heavy. He was watching me as though he were imagining these future interludes, planning and preparing for them.

"I just wish—"

"What do you wish?"

A sudden idea occurred to me and I embraced it before I could think too much about the ramifications; I assumed he'd reject the idea outright, which is why I blurted it. "Heck, let's go all in. If we're going to give it a try, we might as well *really* give it a try. I think we should throw caution to the wind and label each other as girlfriend and boyfriend. Ala, *Have you met Martin? He's my boyfriend. I'm Parker, his girlfriend. We're together in the biblical sense of the word, sans the sacrament.*"

He stared at me for five full seconds, obviously caught off guard by my suggestion, but then he surprised me by reaching forward, and with a sure and smooth movement, pulled me onto his lap. I stumbled and basically fell into him. Meanwhile his hands cradled my face, his thumbs caressed the line of my jaw, and his eyes moved almost reverently from the progress of his fingers to my lips.

"Parker," his voice was a rumbly, growly whisper, laced with warning, "don't say it unless you mean it."

Well, crap. Bluff called.

I licked my lips—a nervous habit—which had the byproduct of turning his aqua eyes darker. He looked...greedy.

"Martin, this is nuts. You don't need or want a girlfriend."

"I want you."

Gah! Right in the feels!

He felt comfortable touching me, that much was clear. But I hesitated to touch him. I didn't want to touch him when he wasn't really mine; because *when* this was over, I wouldn't be allowed to touch him anymore. Then I would have lost something.

Therefore, I crossed my arms over my chest and shook my head.

"Let's talk about our differences," I said, hoping a well-reasoned argument would make some kind of dent in his crazy fixation.

Again, he ground his teeth; his hands slipped away from my face and his arms wrapped around me, as though to keep me from leaving.

"Yesterday, back in the limo," I said, firming my resolve, "and then on the boat, and then when we left the marina, you did this thing where you gave the other guys dirty looks for talking to me."

Martin stared at me, betraying nothing of his thoughts.

"I feel pretty confident in stating that you're…well, you're interested in me and it's not platonic. Therefore, your behavior felt as though you were marking your territory. I've never had a guy do that before, but maybe I'm misreading the situation…?"

He cleared his throat again. "You're not."

"I didn't like it."

"You didn't like it?"

"No. I didn't. It made me feel like, I don't know, like I was Chinese leftovers and you didn't want anyone to sample me."

"I don't want anyone to sample you."

"But I'm not food. I get to say who samples and who doesn't."

"I thought most girls liked it when guys were possessive."

"Really?" I asked this because I really didn't think so; then I shook my head. "No. At least…well, at least I don't think so, not like that. It's like, why would I want to be with someone who doesn't trust me to be loyal? I'm not a buffet. Guys can't sample the lo mein just because I'm standing there. I get a vote in who eats my noodles."

"I trust you," he said quickly, his gaze darting to mine then away.

123

"After Friday night, what you did, I think I trust you more than anyone."

Oh, gah! He sounded so...sincere. I ached for him, because I believed him and it made me sad. How was it possible *I* was the most trustworthy person in his life? How heartbreaking was that?

Unable to help myself and spurred by a sudden desire to touch him, I placed my hands on his shoulders. "Martin, it's just, I don't have much experience with dating or having a boyfriend. I've had one, but he wasn't...well, he didn't count. I'm not really sure how it works—"

"I have even less experience than you."

I glared at him. "That's a lie."

"No. It's not. I've never...," he cleared his throat, "...you're the first girl I've wanted...like this." He sounded enormously frustrated and his fingers dug into my hip and ribs where he held me. When he spoke next it was through gritted teeth. "I just wish you'd be less stubborn."

"You can't always have your way."

"I know that. If I had my way we'd be naked right now in the ocean or...shit, doing anything other than discussing more reasons why you don't think this is going to work."

My instinct was to pacify him, reach forward and soothe his bad temper, promise I would stop being difficult and just give in to the fantasy of this being my reality. But I couldn't ignore reason and logic, even if I was strangely flattered by his caveman displays, possessive impatience, and apparent fixation.

And also...skinny-dipping with Martin = pre-bedtime imagery for the win.

Heat raced up my neck and over my cheeks and I squeezed my eyes shut, gathering a deep breath. I hoped to also re-gather my wits, because right that minute they were skinny-dipping with Martin some hundred yards away in the Caribbean.

"And now you're blushing." He didn't sound pleased about this. He sounded frustrated and resentful.

"What do you expect?" I asked, then opened my eyes. "I'm not used to this. It's going to take me some time to get used to the idea that you're interested in me. For cripe's sake, it's been forty-eight hours and we're not even dating—"

"We are dating. Remember, we're having tacos and soon we're going to have lots of dance lessons." His eyes drifted to the love marks on my neck and he smirked. It was a satisfied, pleased smirk.

A jerk smirk.

"Well, future tacos notwithstanding," strategically and stubbornly, I ignored his reference to dance lessons, "I know I'm not your girlfriend, and even if I were I wouldn't want to be peed on."

Martin choked on air then gave me a squirrely look. "Peed on?"

"You know, figuratively and—for the record—literally. If we got to a place where we became 'involved'," I used air quotes to emphasize *involved*, because it seemed like an odd word, but the most appropriate for the situation, "I don't think I'd be happy with you marking your territory, unless some guy was being inappropriate with me and I sent out the boyfriend bat signal."

He glared at me, his gaze searching. Then he nodded. "Fine. If I go all day tomorrow without...peeing on you," his lips twitched, but he quickly schooled his expression, "if I do that, then you'll come to the party with me tomorrow night."

What should have been a request or a question was once again a declaration. I stared at him. I really hated parties.

But he looked...oddly hopeful.

Oddly hopeful on Martin Sandeke made my heart melt. His expression, plus the feel of him all around me, meant I really didn't have much of a choice.

"Fine." I sighed, trying not to sound like a petulant teenager and *mostly* succeeding. "I'll go."

[11]

STOICHIOMETRY: CALCULATIONS WITH CHEMICAL FORMULAS AND EQUATIONS

M ARTIN DIDN'T PEE on me. In fact, he didn't even look at me or talk to me for most of the day.

Like the day before, the guys were up early practicing, Sam and I assumed our spots on the beach, and they arrived in the early afternoon for food. I left as soon as Ben arrived. He made me feel uncomfortable and icky—and I knew that was on me. I should have been able to ignore him, but I couldn't. So I left.

I milled around the house, exploring, expecting Martin to show up. He didn't. I found the music room—yes, this compound of excess had its own music room, with signed gold records from rock and country music legends lining the walls, signed concert posters, and pictures of a tall, lanky, geeky looking dude alongside several notable musicians and celebrities.

I recognized the geeky dude in the photos as Martin's dad and noted they had the same thick hair and lips. They were likely the same height. But that's where the similarities seemed to end. After inspecting the pictures several times, testing out the baby grand piano —it needed to be tuned—and discovering three beautiful Gibson guitars along the wall, I went back to my room and read.

Then I did some chemistry homework.

Then I took a nap.

Then I woke up on a man.

I didn't realize it at first, because I suffered from post-nap confusion. When I did come to my senses I discovered I was half sprawled on a hard chest, and fingers were playing with my hair, brushing it back from my cheeks and neck, gathering it, twisting it, tugging it lightly.

I stiffened, shot upward, lifted my fists to defend my honor, and found Martin laying on the bed, his hands up like he surrendered.

"Whoa!" His eyes were huge and he gave me a startled smile. "Do you always jump up like that after sleeping?"

"Like what? A badass?" My voice was gravelly, still laced with sleep.

"Yeah, like a badass."

I huffed, let my fists fall to my lap. "No. Only when I find Martin Sandeke on my bed."

"Good to know." His lips twisted to the side and his eyes swept up and down my form. "I'll make sure to wear protection when I'm in your bed."

"You should probably wear it even when we're not in bed."

"I always use protection." He lifted an eyebrow meaningfully.

Pause.

Blink.

Oh...I get it.

Amazingly I didn't blush. I just gave him a half-lidded *I'm not impressed* glare which made him burst out laughing.

"You are such a guy." I gave him a reluctant smile.

"What do you know about guys?" He repositioned himself on the bed, scooching up and placing his hands behind his back against the pillows.

"Admittedly, not much. My dad isn't much of a *guy*."

"What's your dad like?" Martin sounded interested, his face suddenly sober.

"Well, let's see. He's a scientist. He's always losing things. His socks never match. He loves baseball, but he can't play it very well. He tried to get me to play softball. I'd always sneak my Gameboy in my practice bag then hide behind the bleachers and play Dr. Mario instead."

"So he pushed you a lot?"

"No. Not at all. I think he wanted me to do it because he likes cheering for me…to be honest. He's always the one taking pictures, at events, ceremonies, that kind of thing. He's hardly ever in the pictures. I looked back at my high school graduation photos and realized he'd taken over a thousand, but he wasn't in any of them. So I dressed back up in my cap and gown, did my hair the same, and—with George's help—arranged to have a photographer come to the house so we could get some good shots."

"Who's George? Your ex-boyfriend? The one who didn't know how to fool around?"

"No." I glared at Martin, shook my head at his antics. "George is my mom's personal assistant, he's like an older brother to me."

"Hmm…" Martin's eyes narrowed a fraction, considering me, then asked, "Did your dad like that? What you did?"

I nodded, smiling at the memory. "Yeah. He did. He cried actually. Not a lot, just a little. The last time I visited him at work, I saw he'd hung up no less than six of the pictures in his office." I laughed lightly, shaking my head. "He's a goof."

We were quiet for a long moment, sharing a stare. His mouth held a whisper of a smile as though he were living vicariously through my experience and found it a pleasant place to visit. It was…nice. Comfortable. Strange.

I cleared my throat, averted my eyes, finding this nice, comfortable, strange moment more disconcerting than the heated exchanges we'd shared so far. This felt like it could lead to something lasting and normal. We were Martin and Kaitlyn having a conversation, sharing things, like real people did. Not like billionaire playboys did.

"So, what about your dad?" I asked, because I was curious. I knew a lot about Martin's dad because his dad was a genius, sickeningly rich, and seemed to be in the news all the time dating some model or actress.

"My dad..." The smile left his eyes, and the one that lingered on his lips looked false.

"Yes. The man who raised you."

He barked a humorless laugh and his eyes closed. "He didn't raise me."

I studied his features—his full, delicious lips, strong jaw, high cheekbones, and thick lashes—his perfect features. So perfect. I wondered what it would be like to be perfect, or at least seen that way by the outside world. It seemed to me that perfect—the word and all its connotations—might feel a bit like a cage, a defined floor and ceiling.

"Tell me about him," I said, knowing I was pushing.

Martin opened his eyes and the bitterness that had been absent the last few times we'd been together was back. Jaded, jerk-faced Martin.

"He didn't come to my high school graduation."

I blinked at him. "Oh?"

"No. He said later that it was because I wasn't valedictorian, but I think it's because he forgot about it. It didn't rank in his priorities."

"Oh," I said, because I wasn't sure what else to say. His eyes were hooded, guarded, taunting—like he was daring me to feel sorry for him. I wouldn't though. Or, rather, I wouldn't show it.

"He's the smartest man in the world, did you know that? He's taken all the tests, whatever the fuck that means, and overall he's the smartest."

I placed my hand on his thigh and squeezed. "There's more than one kind of smart, Martin."

"That's true," he conceded, his eyes losing focus over my shoulder as he considered my words.

Feeling brave, I added, "I don't think any of those examinations tested for parent-smarts, or priority-smarts, or valuing-your-incredible-son-smarts, because if they did, he would have failed."

His brilliant gaze refocused on mine and I was somewhat surprised to see the bitterness leech out of his expression, leaving only sorrow and breath-stealing vulnerability.

"You're a good person, Kaitlyn." He was frowning at me, like I was a puzzle or a unicorn, like "good people" were the subject of fairy tales.

I opened my mouth, then closed it, then opened it again. "Thank you. You are too, Martin."

His answering smirk looked wry and his eyes moved to my neck, where I still had the purplish marks from our encounter in the cove.

Normal and comfortable conversation gave way to our baseline: sexual tension. His half-lidded stare grew hot, the intensity of it built a fire in the area of my pants. He was forever building fires in my pants. The figurative Bunsen burner forever alight.

"You've never lied to me before," he said, his voice sultry and teasing.

"I haven't lied yet."

"Parker." He gave me a knowing look.

"What?"

"I'm not so good. You know that, remember? You called me a jerk-faced bully."

"Well, so far you've been good to me, as far as I know."

"I'd like to do more good things, better things, if you'll let me..."

I was hot. My cheeks were flushed. I had to measure and regulate my breathing. The soreness between my legs was a lovely reminder of the good things he'd done, but so were the marks on my neck.

"No more hickies," I blurted.

His eyes widened though he grinned. "Why not?"

"Would you like me to give you a hicky?"

"Hell yeah."

I rolled my eyes. "I'm going to call your bluff. I will give you a hicky."

He held his hands out to his sides like he was offering himself to me. "Anytime, lambchop."

"I'll do it on your bottom and I'll make them so big, you won't be able to sit down." I narrowed my eyes and pointed at him.

He groaned like a starving man taking a bite of the most delectable dessert, as though the very thought was more pleasurable than he could process.

I scoffed at him, snorting. *"You're a doofus."*

Then he sat up and scooched to where I sat, one hand sliding up my thigh into the hem of my cotton shorts, his other tucking my hair behind my ear. His eyes felt cherishing and a little lost. The effect of his triple assault—earnest eyes, caressing hands, sexy smile—potent.

"I told you before," he paused, brushed a light kiss over my lips, leaving me breathless as he continued in a low voice, "don't say it unless you mean it."

I lifted my chin for another kiss, but to my surprise, Martin stood from the bed. I watched him, confused by his withdrawal, and wrapped my arms around my middle.

He glanced at me and must have sensed my confusion, because he explained as he walked backward to the door. "It's late, you've been sleeping for hours. You missed dinner, again. I'll get Rosa to bring you a tray before we leave, but we need to get going."

"Going? Where are we going?"

His smile turned smirky and victorious as he said, "To the party of course."

The party.

The bet.

I'd forgotten.

Well...barnacles.

* * *

MARTIN WON THE BET, even though he'd cheated, and therefore Sam was in my room getting me ready for the party. She saw me coming out of my room with my hair in a ponytail, wearing sweat pants, flip flops, and a raggedy stained T-shirt that showed Chuck Norris destroying the periodic table. It read, *The only element I believe in is the element of surprise.*

She didn't think my attire was appropriate.

Therefore she marched me back into my room, made me wait while she found some suitable clothes from her room, then dolled me up. She'd put me in a backless orange and purple paisley halter dress that made my boobs look fantastic. She also scrunched my hair with chemicals, separating my curls and somewhat taming the frizz.

To top it all off, she put makeup on my face. *Again.* It was some kind of personal record, makeup twice in one week. I gave her my resting bitch face while she applied mascara to my lashes.

"The straps of the halter covers your...," her eyes flickered to my neck, "...it covers your love marks."

I grumbled. "Just make me look pretty so I can throw myself off a cliff."

"You are being ridiculous."

"You know I hate parties."

"You didn't complain this much on Friday."

"That's because I had a mission. I had a reason to be there, an assignment. Get in, tell Martin about the plot, get out, go home. This time," I lifted my hands—and my newly painted purple fingernails— then let them drop noisily with a smack on my thigh, "this time I'm window dressing. I'm the paisley curtains."

"This dress looks great on you."

"I know, I'm sorry. You are being so nice. I just need to complain."

I wasn't kidding when I'd said I hated parties.

Hate!

I didn't understand them. They seemed to bring out the worst in people. People laughed too loud, talked too loud, exhibited odd behavior, pretended to have fun when they weren't having fun...or maybe that was just me. Maybe people *did* have fun at parties and I was the weirdo.

Despite my grumpy stance, I had to admit Sam was a miracle worker. I looked good.

We met the boys in the foyer; they were dressed casually in shorts and T-shirts, but they all seemed to have taken special care shaving, administering product to their hair, and applying cologne. It was a variable hurricane of smells—all flavored Proctor and Gamble manly.

Yet some of my surliness receded when Martin looked up and our gazes met. When his eyes widened a little and he appeared to be some degree of blindsided by my appearance. His lips parted and his eyes dropped, moving up and down a few times, blinking.

Sam nudged me and cleared her throat, saying just loud enough for me to hear, "It's not the dress and it's not the makeup, it's you." Then she walked toward Eric, addressing her next comment to him, "This time I want to drive."

"You drove last time."

"Your point?"

He smiled at her, looking handsome and happy, then shrugged. "Fine, drive now, ride later."

She hit him on the shoulder, but she laughed at his double entendre, and walked out the door. Meanwhile Martin pulled his eyes from me and I was a little perplexed to see a mask of boredom slip over his features.

"Hey Ray," Martin said. "You got Parker? Griffin is going to ride with me."

I felt like I'd just been pawned off and had no idea why. I didn't even want to go to this party, Martin had *insisted*, and now he didn't want to ride with me?

Ray glanced from me to Martin, then back again, his raised eyebrows and slightly parted lips betraying his surprise.

"Ssssure," he said, hesitating, frowning his confusion. Martin and Ray exchanged a glance as I fiddled with the pocket of my dress, all the good feelings upon entering the foyer dissipating in the face of this strange exchange. As well, Ben was there and I could feel his slimy eyes on me. I wished my boobs didn't look quite so fantastic in this dress.

Then Ray nodded with sudden vehemence. "I mean, absolutely." He turned a bright smile to me. I was relieved to see how genuine it looked, and he offered me his arm. "I'd love to."

"Thanks." I gave him a tight smile.

Boys were weird and I hated them. Except Ray. Ray was nice.

We left first. He chatted amicably on the drive over, making me laugh with a story about how he fainted in high school when he had to dissect a stingray. He also had a really engaging smile and an openness about him and made me think we were friends, or he was my ally, or I could trust him not to eat my Chinese leftovers even when I wasn't looking.

When we arrived at the house—another sprawling monstrosity, though slightly less sprawling—Ray ran over to my side of the cart and helped me out. We were the first to arrive, so he seemed content to loiter by the cart while we waited for the others.

Ray fit my hand in his elbow and gave me a big grin. "So, you and Martin, huh?"

"I don't honestly know. Doesn't make much sense to me," I admitted, shrugging.

"It makes sense to me." His words were quiet, softly spoken.

I looked up at Ray, surprised to find him looking down at me with equally soft eyes. "You're smart, beautiful—"

I snorted, rolled my eyes.

"Wait, listen, you're not pretty in a conventional way. You're not pretty at all. You're beautiful."

I pressed my lips together and frowned at him, saying flatly, "And I have a really great personality, right?"

He grinned at that, looked like he was trying not to laugh. "Yeah, you do have a really great personality."

"You're nice, Ray."

"No, *you're* nice, Kaitlyn. And you have a nice laugh and a great, weird smile with that cute gap between your teeth."

I mock-scowled at him, pressing my lips together.

He seemed to hesitate as he studied me, debating whether or not to give a voice to his thoughts. He must've decided in favor of the idea because he abruptly said, "You're the girl that guys like us, if we're smart and if we're lucky that is, you're the girl we marry. You're the marriage girl."

My jaw dropped and my eyes bugged out of my head. It took me three or four seconds to find my voice before I said, "What are you talking about?"

"I have two sisters, and I tell them this all the time. Be the marriage girl. Don't be the hook-up girl. Don't be her. She's stupid and shallow.

Yes, she gets lots of male attention, dressing in her sexy lumberjack or sexy nun costumes…for a time. But then she's used up, hardened, disillusioned and desperate, because no one stays with the hook-up girl."

I blinked at him, pulled my hand from his elbow, and backed up a step. "You're disgusting and that's completely misogynistic. What if the hook-up girl is using you just as much as you're using her? What if she's just having fun? This is the problem with society. When a guy sleeps around, he's sowing oats. When a girl does it, she's a hook-up girl."

He held his hands up and shook his head. "I'm not going to defend society, I'm not saying it's right. I'm saying it's biology. It's evolution. It's programmed behavior."

"You do realize I'm nineteen, right? I may never marry. And I certainly won't be getting married any time soon."

"Doesn't matter. Your independence, the fact you aren't actively seeking your MRS degree—that the very idea is repellant—only makes you more of the marriage girl. You're the polar opposite of the hook-up girl."

I growled at him. He laughed at me.

"Listen, I'm not talking about the girl who wants to have fun and a good time with no strings attached. I'm talking about the girl who's looking for a free ride after the ride ends."

I snapped my mouth shut, scowling at him for real, and crossed my arms over my chest. I said nothing, because I knew that girl. Well, I didn't know her, but I'd overheard her plotting with Ben on Friday to drug Martin. *That* was what Ray meant when he was talking about the hook-up girl.

"Ah…I see you know what I mean."

I huffed. "I don't even know what we're talking about anymore."

"You. You're not the hook-up girl, you couldn't be if you tried. You're the girl we marry."

"How lovely for you, especially after you've spent your adolescence and early adulthood making girls like me feel like excrement."

He gave me a shrug that would have been charming ten minutes ago. "I'm just telling the truth. It might not be easy to hear, but that's the way of the world. You are the finest example of the marriage girl I've ever met. You're beautiful. From what I've seen, you're graceful under pressure, smart, capable, and drama free. You come from a family that's historically famous for being brilliant and exceptional. You're nice—like really, really nice—genuine, and you're hilarious."

"You think I'm funny now? Just wait until the party. There will copious pointing and laughing then."

Ray ignored me. "*That's* why you and Martin make sense. Because, if Martin is one thing, he's smart. He may not be nice, but he is fucking sharp as a Katana. He's never had to work for it, he's never had to work for anything. He's bored. He's had his fun. He's over the hook-up girls. He's ready for what's next and you are the Olympic gold medal, the Nobel Peace Prize, the Pulitzer Prize, and the Academy Award of marriage material."

The rest of the carts chose just that moment to show up. I heard Sam's squeals of glee as she and Eric swung around the corner. They parked neatly and tidily in the space next to Ray's. Herc and Tambor were next, followed by Lee and Will, Ben by himself, then Martin and Griffin bringing up the rear.

Meanwhile Ray was looking at me like an older brother might look at his sister, or a father might look at his daughter, after delivering a hard truth about life. Like he was apologizing for the way things were, but not sorry to have delivered the message.

He stepped forward and offered me his elbow. "Did I ruin your night?" His tone was sober and apologetic.

I shook my head, took his offered arm, and said, "No." He hadn't ruined my night because I was going to a party. There was no way to ruin something that was already ruined.

"I've known him forever," he whispered, as the engines of our companions' carts turned off and they spilled out onto the gravel driveway.

"How long?" I asked, careful to keep my voice low.

"Since elementary school."

I nodded, thinking about this, thinking about our bizarre conversation.

"He's kind of crazy about you, Kaitlyn."

My eyes cut to Ray's. His mouth was a grim line. Before I could question him further, the others were upon us and our strange heart-to-heart was at an end.

"Let's go!" Sam slipped her arm in mine and tugged.

Ray let me go with a small smile and a wave, and a look that said, *Let me know if I can help.*

I didn't know quite how to respond to that, what look to give in return. So I turned my attention to the mansion in front of me and the task at hand. I couldn't think about being Martin's marriage girl, not until I was safely through the evening with the odious party at an end.

Then and only then would I examine this new development and try to figure out what, if anything, I was going to do about it.

[12]

LIMITING REACTANTS

Sometimes I hate it when I'm right. Sometimes I love it when I'm wrong.

Let me explain what happened. I'll try to keep it as emotion free as possible for the sake of all the people who can't deal with the ups and the downs, and the drama and the angst. This is because I'm one of those people. I can't deal with the drama. Admittedly, this is likely because I was raised in a drama-free household.

I once tried being dramatic when I was fourteen. My mother told me to add it to the calendar.

We arrived at the house, Sam and I arm-in-arm, the boys behind us. We walked in the door. Martin gave me a curt nod then left. That's right, he walked away. He disappeared into the crowd.

I stood there stunned for about twenty seconds before Sam pulled me closer and yelled over the music, "Maybe he has to use the bathroom or something."

"Or something," I said, feeling gargantuan levels of annoyed and hurt and confused. Boys were so epically strange and obviously placed on the earth to torture girls. Martin's behavior made no sense. I considered trying to sort it out, but ultimately decided the actions of men were beyond my comprehension.

I noted Herc was glued to Ben as they passed and were absorbed into the throng. I'd wondered if Ben would try to drug someone at this party, but now I suspected Herc has been assigned to keep an eye on him.

Sam, Eric—who, let the record show, stayed with Sam—and I took a brief tour of the party. We walked from room to room, surveying the surroundings, getting a lay of the land as it were. To me it looked like a party in a big house and nothing more exciting than that. So...not at all exciting.

The rooms were gargantuan and lavishly decorated and were getting trashed by partygoers. A DJ played loud house music. People were dancing and getting drunk, and talking loudly to hear each other over the music. The majority of the girls were dressed in string bikinis. The majority of the guys were dressed in shorts and T-shirts, or board short swim suits. The pool was huge and wrapped around one side of the house. It had a waterfall and three slides as well as four hot tubs.

Sam said she wanted to go swimming. I hadn't brought a swim suit. She lifted up a bag on her shoulder and informed me that not only had she brought me a swim suit, it was a string bikini. I thought I might die of happiness.

That last part isn't true. I was being sarcastic. Sorry.

Sam and I left Eric on the deck with a promise to return once we were appropriately attired. I numbly got dressed, refusing to look at myself in the mirror, because...why? Why would I do that to myself? Afterward, we walked downstairs. We walked on to the deck.

And I saw Martin kissing a girl.

That's literally how it happened. I took two steps out the door, scanned the space for Eric, and instead saw a leggy blonde with her arms around Martin's neck and her body plastered to his, and her mouth suctioned on his like she wanted to taste his dinner.

I immediately averted my gaze.

Even though you don't feel calm doesn't mean you can't be calm.

"I'm going to kill him." Sam's voice was low with menace.

I gripped her arm to keep her in place and I shook my head, letting her see I considered the whole situation ridiculously futile. I doubted my gaze of acceptance had been very effective because I could feel tears sting my eyes. I turned back to the door and walked away from… all of that hot mess.

I heard her growl at Eric when he started to explain and felt her close behind me as I wove through the crowd. She stopped me when we reached the far end of a huge kitchen.

"God, what an asshole!" I could feel her eyeballing me. "What do you want to do?"

I shrugged and rolled my eyes so I wouldn't cry.

I wouldn't cry.

Nor could I deal with the funnel cloud of feelings that tore through me, because…I just couldn't. I didn't know what to say or do or where to look so I glanced over her shoulder. Several guys were doing keg stands near the largest refrigerator I'd ever seen.

"Kaitlyn, what do you want to do? Do you want to leave?" Sam poked me.

"No," I said. I didn't want to leave. I wanted to find a closet and go chill with myself, calm the rising tide of emotion. "But I do have to go to the bathroom."

"I'll come with."

"No." I shook my head as I spotted Eric hovering behind her, about five feet away. He gave me a grim, apologetic smile. "No. I'm actually fine, I just need a minute. I'll come find you later."

"Kaitlyn…"

"Really, I'm fine," I yelled over the cheering keg standers and lifted my chin toward Eric, encouraging him to rescue me from Sam.

I did need a minute alone. Actually I needed several. Ironically, I was more likely to find alone time here, in this crowd, than I would if Sam and I left the party. She would want to rage against Martin, maybe pack up and leave the island tonight. I didn't want to do that. I wanted to gather my thoughts, leave the party in a few hours, and fulfill my end of the bargain.

Then in the morning, after a very calm, rational discussion with Martin Sandeke, wherein I spelled out all the very factual reasons he and I would never work—for example, how I now hated him with the fire of all the furnaces in hell, and that he was a lying liar who lied when he said he would never hurt me—I would leave the island.

I wouldn't cry.

I wouldn't accuse.

I hadn't really expected any better from Martin, so why should I be surprised now? Just because he gave me an orgasm near a waterfall. So what? It's not like he'd given me a unicorn. It was just an orgasm.

I would *not* cry. I would simply leave.

As soon as I arrived home, I would email my chemistry professor and request a new lab partner. And if I was very careful—and very lucky—I would never have to set eyes on jerk-face Martin Sandeke ever again.

~END PART 1~

ABOUT THE AUTHOR

Penny Reid lives in Seattle, Washington with her husband, three kids, and an inordinate amount of yarn. She used to spend her days writing federal grant proposals as a biomedical researcher, but now she just writes books.

As of 2018, Penny has published 16 novels.

Come find me-
Mailing list signup: http://pennyreid.ninja/newsletter/ (get exclusive stories, sneak peeks, and pictures of cats knitting hats)
Facebook: http://www.facebook.com/PennyReidWriter
Instagram: https://www.instagram.com/reidromance/
Goodreads: http://www.goodreads.com/ReidRomance
Email: pennreid@gmail.com …hey, you! Email me ;-)
Blog: http://pennyreid.ninja
Twitter: https://twitter.com/ReidRomance
Ravelry: http://www.ravelry.com/people/ReidRomance (if you crochet or knit…!)

Read on for:
Penny Reid Book List

OTHER BOOKS BY PENNY REID

Knitting in the City Series

(Contemporary Romantic Comedy)

Neanderthal Seeks Human: A Smart Romance (#1)

Neanderthal Marries Human: A Smarter Romance (#1.5)

Friends without Benefits: An Unrequited Romance (#2)

Love Hacked: A Reluctant Romance (#3)

Beauty and the Mustache: A Philosophical Romance (#4)

Ninja at First Sight (#4.75)

Happily Ever Ninja: A Married Romance (#5)

Dating-ish: A Humanoid Romance (#6)

Marriage of Inconvenience: (#7)

Winston Brothers Series

(Contemporary Romantic Comedy, spinoff of *Beauty and the Mustache*)

Beauty and the Mustache (#0.5)

Truth or Beard (#1)

Grin and Beard It (#2)

Beard Science (#3)

Beard in Mind (#4)

Dr. Strange Beard (#5)

Beard with Me (#5.5, coming 2019)

Beard Necessities (#6, coming 2019)

Hypothesis Series

(New Adult Romantic Comedy)

Elements of Chemistry: ATTRACTION, HEAT, and CAPTURE (#1)

Laws of Physics: MOTION, SPACE, and TIME (#2, coming 2018)

Fundamentals of Biology: STRUCTURE, EVOLUTION, and GROWTH (#3, coming 2019)

Irish Players (Rugby) Series – by L.H. Cosway and Penny Reid

(Contemporary Sports Romance)

The Hooker and the Hermit (#1)

The Pixie and the Player (#2)

The Cad and the Co-ed (#3)

The Varlet and the Voyeur (#4)

Dear Professor Series

(New Adult Romantic Comedy)

Kissing Tolstoy (#1)

Kissing Galileo (#2, coming 2019)